"You're p   easygoing act of yours, aren't you, Chad?"

He laughed. "It's no act, honey. I have a pretty laid-back nature unless I get riled or crossed. But you've got to be tough in this business. The minute you go soft, you go under." He looked at Thunderbolt again. "If need be, you cut your losses."

"But you're dealing with living creatures, not disposable merchandise," Emily told him.

"I don't let myself get tangled up emotionally with my stock." He paused. "Matter of fact, I don't want to get emotionally involved with anything or any*body* right now. I want you to understand that, Emily."

She nodded, understanding perfectly. He'd searched her out to tell her this specifically. "Then you'd better tone down your custom of kissing certain women when your horses win, mister," she replied. "Some might get the wrong idea...."

Dear Reader,

From a most traditional marriage of convenience to a futuristic matchmaking robot, from a dusty dude ranch to glistening Pearl Harbor, from international adventure to an inner struggle with disturbing memories, this month's sensational Silhouette **Special Edition** authors pull out all the stops to honor your quest for a range of deeply satisfying novels of living and loving in today's world.

Those of you who've written in requesting that Ginna Gray tell dashing David Blaine's story, and those of you who waved the flag for Debbie Macomber's ''Navy'' novels, please take note that your patience is finally being rewarded with *Once in a Lifetime* and *Navy Brat*. For the rest of you, now's the time to discover what all the excitement is about! Naturally, each novel stands solidly alone as, you might say, an extra special Silhouette **Special Edition**.

Don't miss the other special offerings in store for you: four more wonderful novels by talented, talked about writers Nikki Benjamin, Arlene James, Bevlyn Marshall and Christina Dair. Each author brings you a memorable novel packed with stirring emotions and the riches of love: in the tradition of Silhouette **Special Edition**, romance to believe in . . . and to remember.

From all the authors and editors of Silhouette **Special Edition**,

Warmest wishes.

BEVLYN MARSHALL
Thunderbolt

Silhouette Special Edition

Published by Silhouette Books New York

America's Publisher of Contemporary Romance

SILHOUETTE BOOKS
300 East 42nd St., New York, N.Y. 10017

THUNDERBOLT

ISBN: 0-373-09665-8

First Silhouette Books printing April 1991

Printed in the U.S.A.

BEVLYN MARSHALL,

a Connecticut resident, has had a varied career in fashion, public relations and marketing but finds writing the most challenging and satisfying occupation. When she's not at her typewriter, she enjoys tennis, needlepoint, long walks with her husband and toy spaniel, and reading. She believes that people who read are rarely bored or lonely because ''the private pleasure of a good book is one of life's most rewarding pastimes.''

OREGON

NEVADA

Sacramento

San Francisco

Pacific Downs Racetrack

Monterey

Fresno

CALIFORNIA

Malibu

Los Angeles

San Diego

Pacific Ocean

MEXICO

Underlined places are fictitious.

Chapter One

Clutching a manila envelope to her chest, Emily Holt left the lawyer's office and descended the dingy staircase. She had to grip the banister to steady herself, and once outside she took a deep breath, inhaling the cool spring air. Rain had begun to fall lightly, but she didn't notice as she walked down the littered street, feeling dazed and disoriented. She'd never had reason to visit this rundown area of San Francisco until today.

The lawyer had informed Emily that her father had died of a stroke. Her pale cheeks were damp now, but from rain, not tears. She had stopped crying for Edmund Holt years ago. She flagged down a cab at the intersection.

"Where to?" the driver asked as she climbed in.

Emily opened the envelope the lawyer had given her and drew out a copy of her father's will. She gave the cabbie the address recorded on the document, and he drove her to a seedy rooming house a few blocks away. Emily stared at it without moving a muscle.

According to the lawyer, her father had resided here for over four years. Discovering that he'd lived about a few miles from her had stunned Emily almost as much as had hearing about his death. Had she bumped into him on a busy street without realizing it? Had they sat side by side on a cable car, two complete strangers? She still pictured Edmund Holt as he had looked when he'd disappeared from her life twenty years before. How had the years changed his appearance? She would never know. Edmund Holt was lost to her forever now.

"You getting out?" the cabbie asked her.

"No," Emily said. "No one I know lives there anymore." She gave the driver her own address.

On the way there he turned on the radio. "I want to catch the last race at Pacific Downs," he said. "I got fifty bucks riding on a sure thing."

Emily almost smiled. Those could have been her father's last words. Edmund Holt had been a compulsive gambler.

"You ever bet on the horses?" the driver asked her.

Emily shook her head very slowly. "Never. But it seems I've just inherited one."

"No kidding? A racehorse?" The driver sounded impressed.

"Actually, only twenty per cent of a racehorse," Emily amended.

"What's its name?"

"Thunderbolt."

"Sounds like a winner to me." He stopped in front of her apartment building on Telegraph Hill. "Thanks for the tip."

"You'd be better off taking your tips in cash," Emily said dryly, handing him one along with the fare.

The cabbie laughed. "That's a heck of a way for a racehorse owner to talk."

"I don't intend to be one for long," Emily replied, slamming the cab door firmly. She hurried down the walk and went into the well-maintained ivory stucco building.

The first thing Emily did when she entered her apartment, even before she took off her coat, was head for the telephone. She dialed the number written on the card the lawyer had given her and nervously twisted the cord around her hand as she waited for someone to answer. She counted ten rings, twelve, fifteen, and was about to hang up when a gruff voice exploded in her ear.

"Yeah?"

"Hello, is this Mr.—" Emily glanced at the card "—Chadwick Barron?"

"This is Moss. Chad ain't here."

"When will he be in?"

"Your guess is as good as mine, lady."

"Could I leave a message for him, please?"

"Hey, whadda ya think I am? His social secretary?"

"This isn't a social call, Mr. Moss. I've been informed that Mr. Barron is the trainer of a horse named Thunderbolt, and I'd like to—"

"Hey, put out that butt before I stick it up your nose!" the gruff voice boomed.

Emily winced. "Excuse me?"

"I wasn't talking to you, lady. I spotted a stable hand lighting a cigarette. No smoking allowed in the barn."

"But I thought I'd reached Mr. Barron's *office*."

"Same thing. Listen, if you wanna see Chad, your best bet is to come by the track during the morning workout. Around five-thirty or six." And with that Moss hung up.

Emily attempted to reach Chad Barron by phone a few more times during the week without success. She considered sending him a registered letter, but the only address she had was the Pacific Downs Racetrack, and she had doubts that the letter would reach him. Besides, even if it did, there was no guarantee Barron would reply. She pictured the horse trainer as a surly old codger with whiskers and a horsey face.

Having no other alternative, Emily resolved to hunt Barron down at the track Saturday morning. She was impatient to arrange the sale of her share of the racehorse with him. She planned to donate the money to a good cause. She wanted nothing from her father now. Nothing!

Emily shivered in the dawn mist and wrapped her trench coat more tightly around her as she approached the track rail. Men leaned along the rail or huddled in tight groups, mumbling to each other as they watched the horses work out. A few of them turned to stare at Emily, making her feel as if she were invading some private club.

A slender young man wearing a corduroy cap broke away from the pack and approached her. "May I help you, ma'am?" he asked in a light Southern accent.

"I'm looking for Chadwick Barron. Do you know him?"

"Sure do." He tipped his cap. "I'm Bobby Lee Halpert. Chad's my uncle."

"I'd like to talk to him about a horse called Thunderbolt."

"He's jogging Thunder right now." The teenager jutted his chin toward the track.

Emily moved closer to the rail as horses galloped past. "Which one is Thunderbolt?" she called over the clump and clatter of hooves.

Bobby pointed to the left. "Chad's taking him round the far turn. The black one."

Emily watched a big dark horse come toward her through the mist, a creature of great energy and power.

"Oh!" she exclaimed. "He's beautiful."

She meant the horse, but as it neared Emily realized she could have said the same about the rider. Chad Barron didn't look at all as she'd imagined him. His hair was as black and shiny as Thunderbolt's coat, and he seemed as powerfully built, dressed in jeans and a dark jersey. He rode with a careless ease, yet so absolutely centered and balanced on the steed that they seemed to be one and the same creature. The mist gave Barron's rugged face a sheen, and a damp lock of his hair clung to his broad forehead. He passed without seeming to see Emily standing by the rail, her face tilted up to him, her lips slightly parted.

But Chad had seen her all right. And it displeased him. He'd told Bobby time and time again not to bring his girlfriends to the back side. They disrupted the routine. This one seemed more sophisticated than Bobby's usual silly fillies, though. Chad narrowed his eyes. Maybe a little too sophisticated. She looked a few years older than his nephew, who was barely eighteen. Definitely out of Bobby Lee's league, he decided.

After he'd worked with Thunderbolt for another ten minutes, Chad led him off the track and handed him over to his assistant, Moss Greene.

"He's changing leads okay now," Chad told the old man. "He got the idea after I made it clear what was expected." Chad stroked the horse's flank. "He could be a fine competitor with the proper training."

"Too bad his last trainer was a horse's ass," Moss said.

"Hey, don't insult our friend here." Chad patted Thunderbolt's rump. "Where'd Bobby go with the girl?" he asked casually.

"Took her back to the barn," the old man replied.

"Dammit, when is that boy going to learn to keep business separate from pleasure?" Chad turned abruptly and mounted his sturdy Appaloosa. He rode back to the barn with a grim expression.

He wasn't surprised to find Bobby and the young woman in his office at the rear of the barn even though it was off limits to visitors. The office, a converted tack room, was furnished with a scarred wooden desk, a sagging leather couch, a few canvas chairs and a coffee maker perched on a dented file cabinet. Incongruously, an elegant oriental rug covered the rough-planked floor. Chad always felt warm pleasure when he gazed at that rug. As a child he'd played on it in his grandfather's house. The house belonged to Chad's father now and he hadn't set foot in it for ten years.

Bobby, about to pour Emily a cup of coffee, looked up at Chad as he stomped in. "The lady was chilly so I brought her here," he explained. "I knew you wouldn't mind, Uncle Chad."

Like hell he didn't. Chad folded his arms across his chest and stared at the lady in question. His hard expression softened somewhat as he took her in. How could he blame Bobby for risking his ire to make her more comfortable? She was lovely, with long curly auburn hair, pale apricot skin, and burnished gold eyes. Chad caught himself waxing poetic and frowned.

"Sorry, miss, but this is a private office, not a coffee shop."

Oh, that voice of his, Emily thought. The husky growl of it seemed to vibrate right through her chest and almost made her tremble. But she refused to be intimidated and sat down on one of the canvas chairs to make it clear that she wasn't. She stared back at Barron, who looked as if he was considering picking her up and tossing her out the barn door. Let him try, she thought.

But Chad, disinclined to lock horns with a pretty woman, turned his glower in his nephew's direction instead. "Better take your new gal someplace else, Bobby Lee. I have work to do."

"She's not my gal." Bobby gave Emily a rueful smile and put down the glass coffeepot. "She's here to see you."

Chad looked at her with renewed interest. "I don't get many female visitors here at the crack of dawn."

"I was told it was the best time to find you. You're not an easy man to track down, Mr. Barron."

Bobby laughed at that. "Or pin down, either, according to a few unhappy ladies Chad left back in Kentucky."

"Don't you have horses to exercise, boy?" Chad asked his nephew, pretending more irritation than he felt.

"I reckon I do," Bobby agreed in a reluctant tone. "Nice meeting you, Miss Holt." He waved goodbye to Emily and left the office.

A silence followed as Chad watched Emily cross her legs, which were encased in opaque black stockings. Legs as long and slender as a yearling's, he mused. A champion's legs. "What can I do for you, Miss Colt?" he asked, thinking how well the name suited her.

"Holt," she corrected. "I'm Edmund Holt's daughter."

Chad's expression became more friendly. "Eddie never mentioned he had a daughter. Not that I know him that well. How's he doing? I haven't seen him round the backstretch lately."

Emily's throat tightened. "He died of a stroke last month."

"I'm sorry." Chad strode across the expanse of worn rug and placed his big hand on her shoulder. "You have my sympathy, Miss Holt."

Emily looked up and saw compassion in his dark, deep-set eyes. She hadn't expected that from such a brusque, rugged man. She didn't want it from him, either, and shifted her shoulder away from his touch.

"The reason I'm here is because my fath—because Eddie bequeathed me his share of a racehorse."

Chad nodded. "Thunderbolt. A fine animal. Great potential. He hasn't really shown his stuff yet but he'll earn his salt with the proper handling and—"

"I'd like to sell my share as quickly as possible," Emily interrupted. She didn't care about the horse's potential.

Chad said nothing for a moment. He moved slowly, deliberately, behind his scarred wooden desk and sat down. "What's the big rush?" he finally asked.

"I have absolutely no interest in horse racing."

Chad raised his thick eyebrows. "You're not a very sentimental gal, are you?"

"What does sentiment have to do with it?"

"Well, your daddy left you something that meant a lot to him and now you can't wait to get rid of it."

Emily sat rigid. "Let me explain something to you, Mr. Barron," she said in an even, expressionless tone. "Edmund Holt walked out on my mother and me when I was six years old. That was twenty years ago and we never saw him again."

Chad wondered how any man could walk out on a little daughter with coppery curls and golden eyes. Poor kid, he thought. Yet there was nothing the least bit pitiful about this determined young woman. Her reserved manner and cool voice gave nothing away. She played her cards close, all right.

"I'm sorry that he died, of course," Emily continued. "He was my father, after all. But since he considered being a father of little consequence, I'm not going to pretend to have an emotional connection with him now."

"Well, that's being honest enough," Chad allowed.

"If there's one thing I am, it's honest."

"Then you're a woman after my own heart, honey."

His husky drawl made Emily stiffen. Was he flirting with her now? It was hard to read him, and all she knew for sure was that she felt uncomfortable being alone with him in this cool, shadowy barn filled with the rich, earthy scents of horses. She felt out of her element.

Chad stood up abruptly. "Come on. We'll go take a look at Thunder."

"That isn't necessary." Emily remained seated and tilted back her head to look at the man towering over her. "I saw you ride him around the track."

Chad smiled down at her. "A fine-looking animal, don't you think?" He hooked his thumbs into the belt loops of his faded jeans. "Wouldn't you like a closer look?"

"Not really," she replied, glancing away from his silver horse-head belt buckle. "I don't much care for horses."

"Is that a fact?" He considered this for a moment. "Well, it takes all kinds, I suppose."

His patronizing tone irritated Emily. "I don't think my lack of interest in horses is that extraordinary."

"I sure do. All the women I know are crazy about them."

"Then you must not know very many," Emily retorted.

A slow smile eased up his lips. "Not that many."

His smirk stated just the opposite to Emily. "Let's get back to business," she said. "Will you buy my share of Thunderbolt, Mr. Barron?"

Chad returned to his swivel chair and leaned back in it. "Now what makes you suppose I'd be looking to do that?" he asked in an easygoing tone.

"Well, you just got through telling me what great potential he had."

"Honey, all the horses I train have great potential or I wouldn't be wasting my time with them." He propped his big, booted feet on the desk. "I got me a string of thirty Thoroughbreds here at Pacific Downs and I own a percentage of each and every one of them. I like the arrangement with Thunder just fine the way it is."

"Exactly what is the arrangement, Mr. Barron?" Emily was tempted to call him "honey," too, but didn't quite dare.

"Five partners, five equal shares," he replied. "But it's a *limited* partnership. I'm the boss when it comes to training, and nobody interferes with the way I run my stable. What I say goes."

If he wanted to be king of his little fiefdom, that was fine with Emily. She wanted no part of it. She smiled politely. "Well, if you won't buy my share of the horse, Mr. Barron, what do you suggest I do?"

"Wait," he said.

Emily did wait—for him to continue. But he didn't. Instead he paid close attention to the way she impatiently recrossed her legs. "Wait for what?" she asked testily after a long moment.

"For Thunder to break his maiden. My bet is that he'll settle down once he does."

"You want him to break a maiden?" Emily shifted uncomfortably. "Does that mean what I think it does?"

"Depends on what you're thinking, Miss Holt." His lean, tan face remained impassive.

She released an exasperated sigh. "Why don't you just tell me what it means!"

"A maiden is any horse, male or female, that hasn't won a race yet," he explained calmly. "Breaking a maiden means winning for the first time. It doesn't have anything to do with sex, *if* that's what you were thinking." He grinned. "Which I reckon you were from the color in your cheeks."

Emily ignored that and willed the color to recede. "What's keeping Thunderbolt from winning?" she demanded. "What's wrong with him?"

"Nothing proper training can't fix," Chad assured her. "If I didn't have faith in Thunder, I wouldn't have claimed him."

"I don't know what that means, either."

"You don't know what a claiming race is?" Chad looked at her with pretend astonishment. "Next thing you're going to be telling me is that you've never been to a racetrack before."

"Never," Emily replied.

But a dim memory floated in her mind—of being lifted from her seat by her father as the grandstand crowd hooted and cheered. *Our horse won, Emmie! You're my lucky charm, baby!* Emily's eyes stung as she blinked away the memory. She concentrated on Chad's explanation of a claiming race.

"When an owner enters his horse in a claiming race," he was saying, "he's putting it up for grabs.

The horse can be bought from him for the established price.''

"But why would anyone risk losing his horse that way?''

"For the purse, of course. The name of the game is winning purses.''

"It sounds so cold-hearted.''

Chad shrugged. "It's a calculated gamble. Part of the business. Win some, lose some.''

"What was Thunderbolt's established price?''

Chad's dark eyes narrowed. "You have any proof that you own a share of him now, Miss Holt?''

"Of course.'' Emily opened her handbag and extracted the papers the lawyer had given her.

Chad took them from her and examined them closely. "Yep, everything's in order,'' he declared, then swung his feet off the desk and swiveled his chair to face the metal file cabinet. He gave it a swift kick. "Drawer always sticks,'' he explained, opening it with a yank.

He pulled out a folder and handed it to Emily. "You'll find all the information you need here, including the names of the other partners. Maybe one of them will want to buy your share. But if you wait until Thunder wins his first race, you might get a better price.''

"What if he *never* wins?''

"Then I'd lose respect for myself as a trainer. But I don't reckon that's going to happen.'' Chad's lazy smile returned.

It was such an infectious smile that Emily couldn't help but match it with one of her own. "No, I can't see that happening either, Mr. Barron.''

Their eyes met and neither of them tried to break the contact as they sent each other a silent message of mutual attraction. Emily's stomach muscles tightened from the tension of it. What next? she wondered. Not that she wanted it to go any further than this one shared look of appreciation. A man like Chad Barron had no more place in her precise, established life-style than a racehorse did. Yet she felt more disappointment than relief when Chad's penetrating eyes left hers and he looked toward the open doorway.

Emily followed his gaze. A skinny old man with a scraggly growth of gray beard was standing there, scowling and scratching his chin.

"What is it, Moss?" Chad asked him.

Emily recognized the man's name from their abrupt telephone conversation. Moss didn't look any friendlier than he had sounded, she observed, as he gave her a squint-eyed appraisal.

Moss turned his attention back to his boss. "You better come take a look at Easy Rider. Leg's blowed up again."

Chad swore under his breath. "Pardon me, Miss Holt," he said. "Why don't you help yourself to some coffee and look at that file I gave you? I'll be back in a little while if you have any questions." He went out with Moss.

As soon as Chad left, Emily relaxed a little and heard, for the first time, the soft subtle notes of electronic woodwind and strings in the background. She recognized it as New Age music. Glancing around, she spotted speakers on the walls and when she walked over to the coffee maker she noted the compact disc player behind Chad's desk. She found both the choice of music and its presence in a barn a little odd and wondered what other surprises Chadwick Barron had in store for her. This thought pulled her up short. Once the business of the racehorse was settled, Emily reminded herself, their brief acquaintance would be ended.

She surveyed the jumble of mugs on the metal cabinet top and selected the one with the fewest number of chips around the rim. Overcoming her natural fastidiousness, she ignored the coffee stains coating the sides and bottom of the mug and filled it with the hot brew. She took a tentative sip. Another surprise—the coffee was delicious.

Returning to her chair, Emily perused the contents of the folder and discovered that Chad had claimed Thunderbolt for twenty thousand dollars. He'd gotten back his money from four investors, including her father. She copied the other three names in her notebook. Each investor had paid Chad five thousand dollars for a share in the horse's future earnings. Emily wondered how her father had managed to come up with that amount. According to her mother, he'd always gambled away his money as quickly as he'd earned it.

The four investors had also agreed to pay for Thunderbolt's upkeep and expenses, Emily noted with dismay. She frowned as she looked over Chad's expense records, scribbled on various scraps of paper. From what she could make of the messy accounting, the horse wasn't cheap to maintain, even when the cost was divided among all the owners.

Yet another reason to sell her share as quickly as possible, Emily concluded. Not only had Edmund

Holt left her with a racehorse that had never won a race; he'd also saddled her with a portion of its monthly expenses.

It would have been better if he had left her nothing at all, she thought. Why interfere with her life now, after neglecting her for twenty years? She resented having to deal with this problem he had willed her, resented that he'd made no effort to contact her while he was alive. Anger gripped Emily's heart, an old familiar anger that she had buried deep within her long ago. It seemed to have gained strength during its long dormancy. How she wished it had never been awakened!

"Have any questions, Miss Holt?"

At the sound of Chad's deep voice, Emily shot up from her chair and faced him, transferring all the frustrated rage she felt for her father to him. "I certainly do, Mr. Barron. What kind of scam are you pulling here?" She waved the folder at him.

"Scam?" He laughed softly. "That's hardly a flattering description of the way I do business."

Emily didn't let his mild response put her off track. "I'd like to know how you ended up owning a share in Thunderbolt without investing one cent of your own money," she challenged.

"I put up the initial capital when I claimed him," Chad pointed out.

"And got it all back from your investors."

"That's right. And what they get in return, is my expertise as a trainer. I'm very good at what I do, Miss Holt."

"That's for sure. You're the only one who isn't risking anything in this enterprise."

"Whoa," he said, raising his hand. Emily observed the calluses on his toughened palm before he lowered it. "I risk my reputation with every horse I decide to train. Without a good reputation and a winning stable, a trainer is worthless. My partners don't pay me a salary. All I take is an equal share of the purse our horses win. That seems pretty fair to me, and I haven't heard any complaints until now."

His voice had a quiet sincerity, and Emily saw a simple honesty in his eyes. There was something about this man that demanded respect and trust. Emily recognized that she had underestimated him. "I apologize, Mr. Barron," she said after a moment. "I don't know enough about your business to criticize the way you run it."

"Apology accepted," he said. "When someone's as green as you, I can't take offense."

His tolerance of her presumed ignorance punctured Emily's pride. "Actually, I do have a certain amount of business acumen, Mr. Barron," she said, feeling compelled to tell him. "I work for Whittle, Whittle and Wang. I'm sure you've heard of that firm."

"Nope. Can't say I have."

"Well, it happens to be one of the most prestigious accounting firms in San Francisco. I'm a manager there."

"Is that a fact?" Chad looked her up and down. "Then you must be pretty good with figures. Maybe you'd like to examine my assets some day." He drawled out the word *assets*.

Emily didn't play along. "What if all I discover is debits?" She tossed the folder on his desk. "You keep very sloppy records, Mr. Barron."

Chad shrugged off the criticism. "I have my own system, and it makes sense to me. My books more or less balance out at the end of the year."

More or less! Emily almost shuddered over the blasphemy of it. She made no attempt to enlighten him about the benefits of exact, methodical bookkeeping, though, since they'd both come to the conclusion that his business was none of hers.

"I took down the names of the other three investors," she told him. "I'll contact them this weekend."

"So you're still determined to sell out?"

"More determined than ever now that I realize owners split the cost of Thunderbolt's upkeep. I've got better ways to spend my hard-earned money than on some fancy racehorse."

Chad couldn't imagine any better way to spend money, but remained silent. He wasn't going to try to convince the opinionated Miss Holt to hold on to her investment. It seemed a shame, though, that she was so all-fired eager to rid herself of her father's legacy. As Chad caught himself thinking of this, he felt a little uneasy. Hadn't he done exactly that himself ten years ago when he broke with his own father?

"I'll walk you to your car," he offered.

"Oh, don't bother. I'm sure you're very busy."

He was. Morning was the busiest time of day for him. Still, Chad was reluctant to say goodbye to her, even though she impressed him as being too fussy and critical. He doubted they had one thing in common.

But he also found her exceptionally easy on the eye. He simply liked looking at her. Nothing complicated about that.

"At least let me walk you through my barn," he said.

They left the office and walked through the shed row, a clay-paved passageway that went around the outer edge of the stalls. Freshly exercised Thoroughbreds were being led up and down the shed row to cool out. They looked enormous to Emily, who had never been so close to horses before, and she appreciated having Chad by her side.

The barn teemed with activity. Grooms bustled about, saddling, bandaging and rubbing down horses, mucking out stalls, filling feed tubs and water buckets. They shouted and joked with each other over the clamor of neighs and snorts and thudding hooves. The rich scents of this strange world filled Emily's nostrils—a ripe combination of straw, oats and linseed; liniment and manure; saddle soap, leather and sweaty horse flesh. Dogs yapped, chickens and ducks clambered about, and Emily had to maneuver a quick sidestep to avoid bumping into a goat.

"Why are all these other animals in the barn?" she asked Chad. It bothered her sense of order.

"Horses like having company," he replied. "Especially at night." His low, husky voice somehow cut through the din without his slightest effort to raise it. "All God's creatures can get mighty lonely at night, you know."

Emily remained silent although she knew that only too well.

"That's why I have music piped into the stalls," Chad continued. "I have a theory that it comforts the horses during those long quiet hours before sunrise. They say music soothes the savage beast, which must be true, because I'm partial to it myself."

Soothes a savage breast, Emily mentally corrected him. But the image of Chad Barron as a savage beast sent a little thrill up her spine and for once she held her tongue.

She spotted Thunderbolt and Bobby heading toward them down the shed row, and she stopped dead in her tracks. How big and black and powerful the horse was! For the first time she noticed a zig-zag strip of white running down the middle of his face.

Chad pulled her forward. "Don't be afraid to get closer to him. Thunder hardly ever bites."

Until then it hadn't occurred to Emily that horses *did* bite. She'd been more concerned about being kicked or trampled. Chad laughed at her wary expression.

"Thunder's got too much class to harm a lady," he assured her.

Keeping her gaze on the horse's alert, wide-set eyes, Emily took a few apprehensive steps toward him. His coat glistened, and she longed to touch him but didn't dare.

"He seems terribly high-strung to me," she said.

Chad patted the colt's elegantly shaped head. "He was a lot more ornery before I started working with him." He turned to his nephew. "Did he hit the ground okay when you exercised him?"

Bobby nodded. "No more cross fire. I don't know what you did when you rode him earlier, Chad, but he's changing leads fine now."

"I just made it clear who was boss." Chad winked at Emily. "That's the whole key to my success, honey," he drawled. "Just show 'em who's boss."

"Horses, you mean, Mr. Barron?"

He kept a straight face. "Them, too."

Emily rolled her eyes. "Your uncle's a master of the double entendre, isn't he, Bobby?"

"I don't know what that means but he sure is a master horseman. Chad's gonna be as famous as Charlie Whittingham some day."

"Bobby Lee tends to exaggerate," Chad mumbled, examining his boots.

Emily found it amusing that despite his cocksure manner, Chadwick Barron was embarrassed to receive compliments. "Have you ever raced these horses yourself?" she asked him.

Bobby laughed. "Chad's too darn big for that, ma'am."

"Thoroughbreds have legs as fragile as your granny's best china," Chad told her. "I'll jog them around the track to get a feel for what's ailing them, but a man my size could do real harm to their pasterns if he didn't know what he was doing." He ran his hand down Thunderbolt's leg. "You weren't designed to carry much weight, were you, boy?"

The horse nuzzled Chad's shoulder, and Emily found herself wishing that he would nuzzle her, too. Thunderbolt, that was.

"He gets his name from that long white marking on his face," she guessed. It had suddenly occurred to her that the marking was shaped like a lightning bolt.

Chad nodded. "With a blaze like that he's destined to be the fastest horse on the track."

"He would be if he'd just stop acting up at the gate," Bobby said.

"We'll cure him of that habit soon enough," Chad declared with his usual calm self-assurance. "You know, Miss Holt is part owner of this fine animal, Bobby."

"Only temporarily," Emily spoke up quickly. "I can't afford to support a racehorse."

"Not many can," Bobby said with sympathy. "Especially when the horse refuses to bring home the bacon." He gently pulled at Thunderbolt's shank. "Come on, boy. Time to do you up."

Emily quickly slid her hand along the horse's side as it passed. The coat felt like silk. Hot silk. She watched, a half smile on her lips, as Bobby led Thunderbolt to his stall.

"It's real easy to get hooked on such a handsome beast," Chad said, observing her closely.

"Oh, no. I'm not the type."

Chad grinned. "Don't be so sure, Emmie."

"Why did you call me that?" she asked sharply.

"Isn't Emily your first name? That's what I read on the ownership papers you showed me."

"Yes. But only my father ever called me Emmie."

"Do you mind if I do? It sounds more friendly to me somehow."

"No, I don't mind," Emily said. Why should she? She doubted that she would ever see him again.

When they reached the end of the shed row she offered her hand. He shook it vigorously. "Goodbye," she said, attempting to free her hand from his big, rough grip.

He wouldn't let go. "I'm real sorry about your dad. Like I said, I didn't know Eddie well, but he had lots of friends at Pacific Downs."

Emily attempted a smile. "I'm sure he did. The racetrack was always his home away from home."

Chad squeezed her hand, then released it. "Take care, Emmie," he told her softly.

She turned abruptly to hide the tears that sprang to her eyes. To be called Emmie again, to hear the name pronounced in a deep masculine baritone, upset her far more than she knew it should. Without looking back at Chad, she hurried down the path lined with whitewashed barns. Head down, hands stuffed in the pockets of her trench coat, she was oblivious to the activity around her.

Leaning against a tall oak outside his barn, Chad watched Emily's purposeful retreat. When her slender figure disappeared from view he felt relief tinged with regret. He knew it would be for the best if he never laid eyes on her again. Right now he didn't have time in his life for a woman like that—the serious kind. Besides, she would never fit into his world.

His world. Chad looked around him, at peace in the midst of the hurly-burly. The fog had lifted and an early-morning glow lit the scene, making everything seem more vibrant.

Chad knew most of the people milling about. Some he would trust with his life; others he wouldn't trust as far as he could throw them. He had a few enemies on the back side but they were far outnumbered by friends.

Smiley the Tout was hanging around as usual, expression glum as always despite his nickname, big ears open for a hot tip that he could sell. One of the track veterinarians, Doc Revera, nodded to Chad as he hurried down the path making his rounds, and Roscoe the horseshoer beeped his horn and waved his beefy arm as he drove by in his beat-up red camper. Feed and tack salesmen were peddling their wares from barn to barn, along with earnest agents hustling mounts for the jockeys they represented.

And everywhere there were racehorses. Their presence filled Chad's senses. He gloried in the sight, the sound, the smell of them. Some were being bathed and brushed outside their stables, and in the sun their coats shone like bronze and silver, copper and onyx. Some were hitched to hot-walking machines, circling round and round as they cooled down after their workouts. As far as Chad was concerned, no other species in the animal kingdom could match a Thoroughbred in grace and symmetry, beauty and power.

Like so many before him, Chad had staked all his hopes and dreams on these creatures. They took up every ounce of his energy, dawn to dusk, seven days a week. He didn't mind. He reveled in his work. He went back to it now, putting all thoughts of Emily Holt aside. For good, he expected.

Chapter Two

Emily hung up her phone Sunday evening, disheartened over the conversations she'd had with two of Thunderbolt's owners. One of them, a psychiatrist, declared himself "insane" for sinking money into a neurotic racehorse that balked at the starting gate. The other, a car dealer, referred to Thunderbolt as a "lemon." Neither of them wanted to buy Emily's share, and she wondered how straight Chad Barron had been with her about Thunderbolt's so-called potential.

More determined than ever to divest herself of such a risky investment, she called the third person on her list.

"Is this Mrs. Florence Feducci?" she asked when a woman answered.

"None other," the woman replied briskly. "Who wants to know?"

"My name is Emily Holt. My father died recently and—"

"Eddie Holt's daughter!" Mrs. Feducci exclaimed with warm enthusiasm. "Why, it's just wonderful to hear from you, sweetie. Your dad was a lovely human being, God rest his soul."

"You knew him?" Emily asked, surprised. The other two partners hadn't.

"I met him at the track a few years ago," Mrs. Feducci replied. "A shame, a real shame that he died so suddenly. When I got back from Florida last week I heard the bad news from Sam Seager. Have you talked to Sam about your father?"

"No."

"Oh, you should. He knew Eddie even better than I did. They were real buddies."

"Actually, I didn't call to talk about Edmund Holt specifically, Mrs. Feducci. I didn't even realize you were acquainted with him. The thing is, I inherited his share of Thunderbolt and—"

"Isn't that nice!" Mrs. Feducci interrupted. "Whenever Thunderbolt races you can think of your father."

But Emily didn't want to think of her father. She'd made a supreme effort to forget him long ago. "The reason I'm calling—" she started again.

And Mrs. Feducci interrupted again. "You want to discuss the horse with me, right? Why don't we get together for lunch? Not only can I fill you in on Thunder, I have lots of fond memories of Eddie that I could share with you."

Emily felt a twinge of jealousy that this stranger had many fond memories of her father while she had so few. At the same time she couldn't find it in her heart to say no to the invitation. The woman sounded so sincere and well meaning.

"All right," Emily agreed. "Would tomorrow be good for you?"

"Sure. Why don't we meet at Gaylord India? Not the restaurant in Ghirardelli Square, but the one at Embarcadero Center."

"That's convenient for me," Emily said. "I work in the financial district."

"I know. That's why I suggested it."

"You know where I work?" Emily asked, amazed.

"Sure. Eddie told me."

"*He* knew where I worked?" Her amazement increased.

"Your dad kept tabs on you, sweetie," Mrs. Feducci told her. "But I'd rather talk to you about him in person. See you at Gaylord around twelvish."

"How will I recognize you?"

The woman laughed throatily. "Just look for the most conspicuous broad in the joint."

The next morning Emily kept checking her office clock, anticipating her luncheon date with Mrs. Feducci. She left for the restaurant at ten of twelve, and as she walked down Sacramento Street a cloud of apprehension enveloped her. She wasn't sure she wanted to discuss her father with a stranger. Until last week, she hadn't talked about her father to anyone for years.

When Emily entered the restaurant she saw a large, middle-aged woman dressed entirely in purple, from the top of her turban hat to the tips of her suede boots, sitting at a table for two. She was certainly the most conspicuous person in the place.

Emily approached the table with caution. "Mrs. Feducci?"

"Emily! You're just as pretty as your father described you." She motioned for Emily to sit down across from her. "Please call me Flo. I feel as if I know you, sweetie. Eddie talked about you all the time."

Emily found this incomprehensible. "He hadn't seen me since I was a child."

"He watched over you, Emily. From a distance. But pride kept him from getting in contact with you."

"You mean he was too proud to have anything to do with his own flesh and blood?" Emily's voice cracked a little.

"That's not what I meant at all! See, Eddie didn't want you to know what a failure—" Flo hesitated. "Maybe he wouldn't like me discussing his personal business with you, sweetie."

Not sure that she wanted to discuss it, either, Emily made no effort to prompt Flo to go on. She looked down at her menu.

"I recommend the rogan josh," Flo said. "Best I've had since I was in India."

"You were in India?" Emily asked politely, feeling more comfortable with small talk.

"You name it, I've been there," Flo boasted. But she didn't sound too happy about it. "After my husband passed away, I got a bad case of wanderlust. I felt like a boat without an anchor and just floated around from place to place. It was as if I was searching for a chunk of me that was missing."

"I felt the same way when I lost my mother," Emily said, forgetting to stick to small talk. "We were very close. She died in a car crash when I was eighteen."

"Poor kid." Flo reached across the table and patted Emily's hand. "Now with your father gone you're an orphan."

"I'm a little old to be considered an orphan." Emily picked up her water glass and took a sip. "Besides, I never really had a father."

Flo nodded sympathetically. "Eddie always regretted deserting you like that."

"Not enough to come back," Emily retorted. "Did he think leaving me his share of a racehorse would make up for what he did?"

"I'm sure he didn't think anything could make up for that," Flo said in a mollifying tone. "But Thunderbolt *is* a magnificent creature. Wait until you see him."

"I already did. When I went to talk to his trainer."

"Ahh, Chad Barron." Flo rolled her eyes. "A magnificent creature in his own right."

The vivid image of Chad riding Thunderbolt through the mist flashed in Emily's mind, as it had many times since Saturday morning.

"So what did you think of him?" Flo asked.

"He seemed too confident that his way was the only way of doing things."

Flo waved away that criticism. "Most trainers tend to be a little arrogant. It comes with the territory."

"A little? Hah! With an ego Chadwick Barron's size, I'm surprised there's room in his barn for the horses."

Flo chuckled. "Big man, big ego. The important thing is that Chad's good at what he does, Emily. He's one of the best trainers in the business. He once claimed a horse named Last Prayer and won the

Preakness with it.'' Declaring this, she leaned back and waited for Emily's reaction.

It was a mild one. ''The Preakness? That's some sort of special race, isn't it?''

''Just one of the most prestigious in the country! I can see that you've got a lot to learn about horse racing, sweetie. But don't worry. Just stick with me and I'll show you the ropes. We're partners, after all.''

''That's what I wanted to talk to you about, Mrs. Feducci.''

''Flo,'' she corrected.

''I wanted to know if you'd like to buy my share of Thunderbolt, Flo.''

''You want to *sell?*'' Flo's face sagged with disappointment. ''If your father were alive, that would break his heart. The only two things he cared about were you and that horse.''

Emily could believe that he had cared about the horse. But not about her. ''If you're not interested I suppose I can put an ad in the paper or—''

''An ad in the paper?'' Flo cried. ''This is a Thoroughbred, not a used car! And who said I wasn't interested?''

''Are you?'' Emily looked at her hopefully.

''I'll think about it,'' Flo said. She hailed a passing waiter. ''Hey, what do you have to be to get served in this joint? A maharaja?''

When the waiter began to apologize profusely, Flo told him she was just kidding, then ordered for both herself and Emily. She talked a blue streak during the meal—all about her journey to India, her African safari, her visit to the Great Wall of China. She didn't mention Eddie Holt again or make another reference to Thunderbolt. When the check came she snatched it up before Emily could.

"My treat," she insisted, placing some bills on the table. "I'll get back to you next week about Thunderbolt, but I hope you change your mind by then."

"I won't," Emily stated firmly. "I don't want to have anything to do with horse racing."

"Or your father," Flo said sadly.

"That's right. He loved gambling more than he loved his family."

"Gambling can be a disease, you know," Flo said. "Like alcoholism, some people are susceptible to it. They don't want it to control their lives, but it does."

"Then he should have gotten help," Emily said without a trace of sympathy in her voice.

"Easier said than done, Emily. His problem caused him a lot of pain."

"Well, he caused my mother too much pain for me to care about *his!*"

"Okay, okay, we won't talk about him. I can see it upsets you," Flo said.

And they left it at that, parting outside the restaurant.

That night Emily awoke from a dream. She rolled over, looked at the digital clock on her night table, and groaned—4:16. She attempted to go back to sleep, but the harder she tried, the more difficult it became. Giving up, she switched on the lamp. Her gray and white cat, Sachet, turned to give her a reproachful stare from the foot of the bed.

"Sorry," Emily said. Hoping the cat would come cuddle against her, she made the lip smacking sound that Sachet liked to hear. But he ignored her.

Feeling rebuffed, Emily sat up, fluffed her pillow and placed it against the headboard. She picked up the magazine on the night table and turned to an article about long-term investments. She couldn't concentrate on it, though. Her dream kept intruding.

Emily rarely remembered dreams, but this one had disturbed her, and the details remained vivid. She had been walking through a dense fog, on a road that was unfamiliar to her. She couldn't see more than a foot ahead and had stretched out her hand, afraid she might bump into something and get hurt.

And then she heard a sound in the distance—galloping hooves coming closer and closer. Sensing danger, she jumped from the path to get out of the way and fell into a ravine. Crouching there, she waited for the intruder to pass. And as it did she caught a glimpse of it through the fog. It was a centaur! Even now, with the light on, Emily felt the hairs on the back of her neck stand up. The centaur had been half black stallion, half Chad Barron.

How silly, Emily thought, impatiently tossing aside the magazine and throwing off the covers. She didn't put much stock in dreams or in anything intangible. She considered herself too rational and practical. She got up and went to the kitchen. The moment she opened the refrigerator door, Sachet joined her. Emily poured some milk in his saucer, grateful for the company.

"I don't like having my sleep disturbed, either," she told her pet as she heated up some milk for herself. "I shouldn't have had that spicy Indian food for lunch."

As Emily sipped her soothing drink, she thought about her meeting with Flo Feducci. She wished she had asked Flo more questions about her father. Per-

haps if they got together again, she wouldn't find
talking about him so uncomfortable. She just needed
a little time to get used to the idea. It seemed so odd
that his death had somehow brought her closer to him.
So odd and sad.

When she returned to her bedroom she began pacing. The milk hadn't made her any sleepier. She decided to do something constructive until it was time to
get ready for work. But what?

Emily looked around her pale blue bedroom. It was
neat as a pin, as all five rooms of her co-op apartment were. Perhaps her dresser drawers needed to be
reorganized, she thought. She opened each one.
Everything was in perfect order. Her lingerie was
carefully folded in silk-lined, scented bags. Her silk
scarves were arranged by color and folded with geo-
metric precision. So were all her sweaters, many of
which were of the finest cashmere.

As Emily went through her drawers she felt proud
that she made enough money to afford a few personal
luxuries. Even as a child she had appreciated fine
things, just as her mother had. They'd admired them
from the distance of shop windows.

Emily pressed the soft sweater she was refolding to
her cheek and gazed at her mother's photograph on
the dresser. How she wished that her mother had lived
to see her successful. More importantly, she wished
her mother could have shared the benefits of her success. It would have been the best luxury of all.

Poor woman, she'd always worked too hard for too
little, Emily thought grimly as she replaced the sweater
and slammed shut the drawer. When Edmund Holt
deserted his wife, Mrs. Holt had been ill-prepared to

earn a living. She had barely managed to support herself and Emily through a variety of low-paying jobs.

Had her father ever made inquiries about how they were faring? Emily wondered. Had he known that his daughter had grown up in relative poverty. If so, had he given a damn?

Emily opened the bottom drawer of the dresser and knelt down to delve into it. Unlike the others, it actually needed to be put in order. She sifted through it, pushing aside high school and college mementos, souvenirs from vacations she'd taken during the past few years and a box containing racing medals she'd won as a teenager.

The sight of this box made her pause a moment as she recalled the glory of winning. But then she continued her rummaging, finally admitting to herself that the entire project of straightening drawers had been a ruse so that she could get to the bottom of this one. There was something in this drawer that she should have thrown away years ago.

Emily almost panicked when she couldn't find it. But then she spotted it—a white envelope pressed against the side of the drawer. She took it out and stared at it, remembering the day she had sealed the envelope and sworn to herself that she would never look at its contents again. She had been twelve when she'd made that pledge.

And now she broke it by breaking the seal. Her heart knocked against her chest as she extracted a glossy postcard. It depicted the grandstand at Saratoga, packed with cheering spectators. The brown oval of the racetrack, with its island of green, was in the background. She turned the card over. Her father's handwriting blurred before her eyes but it didn't matter. The four lines he'd jotted down were engraved on her heart.

"Dear Emmie, I'll come home as soon as I win back my losses. Be a good girl for Mommy. Daddy loves you."

For years Emily had slept with the card tucked under her pillow. And she had spent many hours examining the picture with a magnifying glass, hoping to spot her father in the grandstand crowd even though she knew he wasn't there. When she'd finally grown up enough to accept that he wouldn't be coming home again, despite his promise on the back of the card, she'd still been unable to throw it away. Instead, she had buried the postcard in an envelope.

Now Emily was happy she had saved it. After all, it was all she had to remember her father by. Her mother had torn up all photographs of him and disposed of any personal effects he'd left behind. It occurred to Emily that he must have left personal effects behind at the rooming house. She suddenly felt a strong need to find out what had happened to them and decided to look into the matter.

Pacific Downs Racetrack was located less than ten miles outside San Francisco. The city might as well have been on a different planet as far as Chad was concerned. He had neither the time nor the inclination to visit San Francisco, but on this particular Tuesday he drove in for the sake of his mother. Her birthday was coming up and he wanted to buy her something nice. Chad considered his mother a super lady with the patience of a saint. How else could she have put up with his father for over forty years? Chad viewed his father as a tyrant and hadn't spoken to him since leaving home.

While he was in the city Chad figured he'd kill two birds with one stone. He'd found someone willing to buy Emily Holt's share of Thunderbolt and since she was in such a hurry to sell, he'd brought the necessary papers for her to sign. He parked his Jeep in the financial district and went directly to the Whittle, Whittle and Wang offices.

When Chad got off the elevator, the receptionist at the front desk stopped talking on the phone, the secretary seated behind her stopped typing, and the two women by the copy machine stopped chatting.

"Nice day," he remarked as a general greeting.

"Now it is," the receptionist replied. The other women laughed. "How can I help you, sir?"

"I'm looking for Emily Holt."

One of the women by the copier stepped forward, smiling pleasantly. "She's with another client at the moment. I'm Ms. Holt's assistant and I'd be happy to help you."

"Thank you, but this is a personal matter," Chad told her. "I'll come back later."

"No!" came the chorus as he made a move to press the elevator button.

"You can wait right here," the receptionist added, indicating the sofa beside her desk.

Four pairs of eyes avidly watched as he sat down, folded his arms across his chest and stretched out his long legs. Chad wished they would all go back to what they'd been doing before he'd arrived.

A few minutes later he was relieved to see Emily coming down the hall. She was with a man in a dark pinstripe suit. Chad didn't much care for pinstripe suits. Or any other kind, for that matter.

Emily was also wearing a suit, but she looked great in hers, Chad conceded, even though the skirt was a little longer than he would have liked it. Her beige jacket had padded shoulders, and the cut accentuated her slender waist. Chad wasn't sure that he cared for the way she'd arranged her coppery hair in a neat coil at the nape of her neck. But he approved of her big hammered gold earrings because they matched her eyes. It occurred to Chad that this was the most attention he'd paid to women's fashion in a long time. Of course, most of the women he saw every day wore rough denim work clothes.

The moment Emily spotted Chad her pulse rate shot up. A prickly heat suffused her chest and neck, and her palms began to sweat. She felt silly about this overreaction and proceeded toward the cause of it as if nothing were amiss.

"Mr. Barron, what brings you to W, W and W?" she asked in a cool, smooth business voice.

"Why, you of course," he replied, slowly rising to his full height.

He looked even taller and more muscular to Emily in this staid office setting, dressed in a soft buckskin jacket, a red flannel shirt and jeans. All he needed was a Stetson hat and a cigarette dangling from his wide mouth and he could have posed for a Marlboro ad, Emily thought.

The man beside Emily cleared his throat, reminding her of his presence. She automatically began the introductions.

"Chad Barron, I'd like you to meet..." Emily searched her mind but drew a complete blank. She couldn't remember her client's name for the life of her. To make matters worse, he was more than a client. They had been dating for a few months.

"Roger Molby," he said, breaking the awkward silence and sounding more than a little miffed.

"Of course!" Emily forced a laugh. "Honestly, Roger, there are times when I forget my own name." She touched his arm in apology.

Chad's eyes narrowed when she did that. Not that it was any of his concern who she touched, he reminded himself.

Molby smiled at him, displaying perfect teeth. "Nice to meet you," he said, then dismissed Chad with a turn of his head. "Well, Emily, I think we spent a highly constructive hour together. Until I began working with you, I never realized how exciting financial planning could be." He patted Emily's shoulder as Chad watched. "Are you sure you can't have lunch with me?" he asked her.

"Not today, Roger. I have something to do at noon."

"I was hoping to take you for a drive in my new Lamborghini."

"Some other time," Emily said.

Chad moved a few feet away to push the elevator button for the man, then leaned against the wall and casually listened to the continuing conversation.

"But it's such a lovely day," Roger persisted. "We could take a spin down the coast."

"That sounds great, but I really don't have the time today."

Roger became a bit petulant. "You can't make time for one of your best clients, Emily?"

"Not today, Roger," Chad's deep voice boomed in. "How many times does the lady have to say it? She might as well be shouting down a well." The elevator doors opened, and he gestured toward the waiting car. "Right this way, sport."

"I haven't concluded my conversation with Ms. Holt yet, Barron. A *private* conversation, I might add."

What a pompous ass, Chad thought. "Take your time," he said genially. "I'll hold the door open for you."

"Oh, why don't you go ahead, Roger? I know how busy you are," Emily urged. "I'll call you after I've checked my calendar, and we'll make a date for lunch, okay?"

"Well, all right," Roger said, slightly mollified. He walked past Chad, ignoring him completely, and stepped into the elevator.

"Have a safe trip down," Chad said, releasing the hold button. The doors closed on Roger Molby, and Chad grinned. "That was one persistent joker."

"Roger happens to be a very nice man," Emily said in his defense. It sounded a little half-hearted, though.

"Nice? What's so nice about badgering a woman for a date?"

"He wasn't badgering me exactly. And it's really none of your—" Emily stopped herself, noticing how avidly she and Chad were being observed by office personnel. "Why don't we go into my office, Mr. Barron?"

Once there he looked around, taking in the putty-colored walls, gray carpeting and upholstery, and utilitarian furnishings. "Sort of a sterile environment, isn't it?" he commented.

"What did you expect? Horses and goats and geese running around?"

"No, but a window sure would help. Hell, I'd get claustrophobia stuck in here all day."

Sometimes Emily did feel a bit claustrophobic when she'd put in a long day, but she wasn't going to admit that to Chad. For some reason she wanted to impress him.

"Except for the executive suites, I have one of the largest offices in the firm," she boasted, although it seemed to have shrunk in size now that Chad Barron was in it.

"Then I hope the rest of the bean counters who work here are midgets," he said.

"I assure you they're not," Emily replied in an even tone. "And accountants don't appreciate being referred to as bean counters."

"I'll try to remember that," Chad said, flashing his grin. "Are you going to ask me to sit down?"

"Please do," Emily said, gesturing to a chrome and leather chair. She perched on the edge of her desk, wishing his presence didn't make her so nervous. "So why are you here?" she asked him point blank.

"I brought you good news. I found a buyer for your share of Thunder." He took a folded paper out of the inside pocket of his jacket and handed it to her.

She didn't look at it but stared at him instead. "That was fast."

"I made a few phone calls. Easy as pie. All you have to do is sign on the dotted line, transferring ownership."

Emily unfolded the form. A certified check was paper-clipped to it, made out in the amount of six thousand dollars.

Chad noticed her frown. "That's a fair price. In fact, more than fair considering Thunder hasn't shown his stuff yet."

"I was only expecting five thousand," Emily admitted. "But I'm afraid I can't accept this offer, Chad."

"You've changed your mind and decided to hold on to your inheritance?"

Emily shook her head. "I asked Flo Feducci to buy my share yesterday and agreed to wait for her answer."

"No problem," Chad said. "Just give her a call and tell her about this other offer. Either she'll come back with a better one or bow out."

"But she wanted some time to think about it. I don't want to pressure her. I like her."

"Hell, I like Flo, too," Chad said. "But this is business. And you know what a bird in hand is worth."

"It's just that..." Emily hesitated. "It's just that Flo was my father's *friend*. And I'd feel better having someone who knew and liked Edmund Holt take on his share of Thunderbolt."

Chad raised his eyebrows. "I thought you weren't sentimental about your dad."

"I'm not," Emily insisted. But confusion made her less certain than she sounded. Why didn't she simply take the check and end the matter? she asked herself. Yet she couldn't. She gave it back to Chad. "I'm sorry, but I can't accept this offer right now. Maybe next week."

"Maybe it won't exist next week," Chad pointed out.

"I'll take that chance."

"I thought you disapproved of gambling, Miss Holt." Chad's look was sly and teasing. "Maybe you're not as straitlaced as you seem."

"Straitlaced?" Emily smoothed down the bodice of her close-fitting jacket. "What an old-fashioned word."

"I'm an old-fashioned guy," Chad told her.

"Yes, I do believe you are," Emily said after a moment. "You act as if you just stepped out of the nineteenth century, when men were men and all that."

"Is that a compliment or are you poking fun at me?" He smiled confidently, not at all concerned with the possibility of being ridiculed.

"It was just a simple observation," Emily said. His self-confidence was rare in modern men, she thought, or at least in the ones she knew. Chad seemed so content to be exactly who he was, without pretensions or excuses.

"Well, I reckon that concludes our business," he said, returning the transfer papers and check to his jacket pocket.

Emily felt a twinge of regret that he was leaving, yet she had no reason to ask him to stay. "Thanks for coming in person," she said. "I'm sorry you went to the trouble for nothing."

"No trouble at all. I had to come into the city anyway. I'm hoping to find a gift for a very special lady."

"Really?" Emily forced a little smile. And here she'd been flattering herself into thinking that he'd been treating *her* specially. "Well, good luck in your search."

"I'll need it. I never know what to buy my mother for her birthday."

His mother? Emily's smile became more genuine. "I'm sure she'd love anything you gave her, Chad."

"Yep, mothers are like that. But I want to buy her something unique." He paused, giving Emily an appraising look. "You look like a gal with real good taste. Why don't you come help me? If you do, I'll treat you to lunch."

"I can't, Chad. There's something I have to do during my lunch break."

"Oh, I thought that was just an excuse to get rid of Ralph."

"Roger," Emily corrected. "And I wasn't making up an excuse. I have to go to the rooming house where my father lived to collect his personal belongings." Her shoulders sagged a little. "Someone should do it, and I guess I'm the one."

"That's not something you want to do alone, Emmie. I'll come with you."

Oh, dear—he'd called her Emmie again, and again it caused her eyes to grow moist. Funny, she thought, how a little thing like that could set her off. "I can handle this on my own, Chad," she said.

"I'm sure you can. But now that I'm here you don't have to." He stood up before she could protest further. "Let's go," he said.

Emily's heart suddenly felt a lot lighter. She had been dreading going there by herself.

Chapter Three

Chad parked his Jeep in front of the rooming house, a three-storied Victorian building in bad need of a paint job. It looked even more shabby to Emily in the glare of the noonday sun. They got out and walked up the crumbling walk.

"Watch out for that loose board," Chad said, lightly gripping her arm as they climbed the sagging porch steps.

Emily appreciated his caring gesture even though it had been automatic. Watching out for others seemed to be second nature to him.

She hesitated at the front door, which was ajar and hanging askew. "I don't even know who to talk to here," she said.

"We'll find out."

Chad ushered her inside a dimly lit foyer. The odor of fried food permeated the atmosphere and a loud TV could be heard from behind the door at the end of the hall.

"Let's try there," Chad suggested.

Emily nodded, aware that she was letting him take charge, which wasn't like her.

Chad knocked loudly to be heard over the sounds of the TV. A few minutes passed before an elderly man answered.

"You're interrupting my favorite soap," he groused.

"Sorry to disturb you," Chad said. "We're looking for the person in charge of this building."

"I own it," the man replied. "Name's Glick."

"Well, Mr. Glick, our visit has to do with Eddie Holt."

"Dead," Glick said. "Stroke. Went like that." He snapped his fingers. "Happened last month."

"Yes, we know," Emily spoke up softly. "I'm his daughter."

"Sorry. Didn't know Eddie had any relatives. Never mentioned them."

Emily's face registered no surprise. "What happened to his belongings?"

"You mean his clothes and stuff? Got rid of them. Had to clear out the room for a new boarder."

"You threw away all his things?"

"Hey, there was nothing of value."

Emily had assumed that. Still, her disappointment was great. She had wanted to see her father's possessions. She had wanted to touch them, hoping they would give her some sense of connection with him.

Glick noticed her stricken face. "I didn't think anybody would be coming around to claim Eddie's things, miss. Only visitor he ever had was a racetrack pal name of Seager."

"It doesn't matter," Emily said even though it did. Then she forced herself to ask the one question that had been heavy on her mind. "Did my father...did he die alone in his room?"

"No, it happened at the track. Seager told me he was sitting right next to Eddie when he keeled over. And then he was gone. Like that." Glick snapped his fingers again.

"And he was with a friend," Emily said in a barely audible voice. This comforted her.

"How can we get in contact with Mr. Seager?" Chad asked.

"Can't help you there. Told you all I know." Glick began inching his door shut. "Shame Eddie died. Kept to himself and always paid his rent on time. Gotta go now."

"Well, thank you," Emily said as he closed the door in her face. She had no further questions to ask him, anyway. Head bowed, she turned and hurried out of the musty hallway.

Chad followed her into the sunlight. He took her arm again as they went down the dilapidated steps. "I'll ask around the backstretch and try to locate this Seager fellow," he offered.

"Please don't bother," Emily said. She knew she could reach him through Flo if she wanted to. Which she didn't.

Chad let the matter drop. After all, Eddie Holt had broken all ties with his daughter, and the way Chad figured it, her father didn't deserve her devotion now that it was too late for the man to make amends.

"Want me to drive you back to your office?" he asked Emily. "Or do you have time for lunch with me?"

She glanced at her watch. "I have the time but not much of an appetite, I'm afraid. How about a stroll in Golden Gate Park instead? I could use some fresh air more than food right now."

"A walk in the park sounds fine with me," Chad said even though he was starving. He figured suffering a few hunger pangs was a small price to pay to remain in Emily's company for a while longer. Not that he wanted to get further involved with her. He just couldn't help feeling a little sorry for her. She had looked so darn forlorn when she'd asked the taciturn landlord about her father.

"But I've forgotten all about your errand," Emily said when Chad opened the door of his Jeep for her. "I don't want to keep you from it."

His errand? Chad had all but forgotten about it, too. "I can go shopping later," he said.

"Here's an idea. Let's go to Fisherman's Wharf instead of the park. I may not be hungry but you probably are. You can get great food at the outdoor stalls, and we could look around for your mother's gift while we walk."

"You're on," Chad said. He admired Emily's efficient thoughtfulness almost as much as he admired her legs as she swung them into the Jeep and tucked her skirt around them.

Fisherman's Wharf bustled with activity. Chad bought a fresh crab cocktail in a paper container and consumed it as they walked. He didn't mind. He rarely had time to sit down to a meal and usually ate on the run.

They paused on the pier to watch fishing boats being unloaded and to admire the view. The Golden Gate Bridge glowed orangy red in the distance, and the day was so clear that the purple Marin hills were visible beyond the bridge.

Emily deeply inhaled the salty air as she gazed at the bridge. "I feel much better now. I really love this city."

"Are you a San Francisco native?" Chad asked, paying more attention to her pert profile than the view.

"Oh, no. I got transferred here a few years ago. I grew up in a small town in Massachusetts. What about you?"

"Born and bred in blue-grass country."

"That's right. I recall your nephew mentioning something about all the unhappy ladies you left behind in Kentucky."

Chad smiled. "The only lady I'm aware of who's still unhappy is my mother. She didn't much appreciate her only son leaving the farm to go west."

"Oh, you're a farm boy?"

"That I am," Chad replied, neglecting to mention that Sunny Hill Farm was one of the most prestigious horse-breeding establishments in America.

"What made you leave home?" Emily asked him.

"It was time I went out on my own. My old man and I don't get along." Chad turned away from the view. "What do you say we go look for that gift now?" He didn't feel comfortable when talk turned personal.

Emily took him to an imports bazaar packed with everything from china and gourmet foods to jewelry and antiques. He chose a carved jade bird for his mother. Emily thought it was an exquisite gift, one she herself would have treasured. He paid for it in cash and made arrangements to have it sent to Kentucky.

"You have excellent taste and didn't need my help," Emily told Chad when they left the bazaar and walked down the block to his Jeep. "And you made up your mind so quickly." The jade bird had been expensive but he hadn't hesitated for an instant after he'd spotted it.

"I usually know what I like the minute I see it," Chad replied. He gave Emily a measured look.

"Some people aren't so quick to trust their impulses," she said, breaking eye contact with him. "They need time to shop around and compare."

"Are you the type of gal who likes to shop around and compare?"

His husky voice sounded insinuating to Emily. "I don't have much time for that," she replied a bit sharply. "And I should be getting back to work now."

Chad laughed as she hurried up the street. In a few long strides he caught up with her. "I didn't mean to rile you, Emmie."

"You didn't," she replied coolly.

"Seems I did," he insisted. "It's mighty easy to get your dander up. You remind me of Rosie."

Emily didn't appreciate Chad comparing her to another woman. "Who's she?"

"A chestnut filly in my stable."

Emily appreciated Chad comparing her to a *horse* even less.

"Rosie's got a skittish streak in her same as you," Chad told her.

"I'm not skittish," Emily protested, picking up her pace again. "Just worried about being late for my afternoon appointments."

"Don't worry. I'll get you back to your office in no time flat."

Chad succeeded in doing exactly that by driving up and down the hilly San Francisco streets at a speed that Emily considered imprudent. Not wanting to be accused of being skittish again, she didn't object. Instead, she sat silently with her hands and lips clenched. Yet when he double parked in front of her office building, she felt oddly disappointed that their bumpy ride had ended.

"Thanks for coming to the rooming house with me, Chad."

"Don't mention it. That's not the sort of neighborhood you should visit alone."

"Well, I won't be going back there."

"Too bad about your dad's things."

Emily sighed. "It doesn't matter. I was just curious to know if he had . . ." She let the sentence drift off with a sigh.

"Had what?" Chad prodded gently.

"Kept any remembrance of me. Now I'll never know."

"He probably had a framed picture of you in his room," Chad said to comfort her.

But Emily shook her head. "I doubt it very much. All Edmund Holt ever cared about was betting on the horses. How befitting that he should die at the track." She laughed harshly.

"Bitterness doesn't suit you, honey."

"That's all he left me."

"He left you his share in Thunderbolt," Chad reminded her.

"Which I don't want."

"Then why didn't you accept the offer I brought you today?"

"I explained why."

"Oh, right. Because you're waiting for Flo Feducci's answer. I think there's more to it than that. Deep down you don't want to let go of that part of your father."

"I didn't realize that horse trainers were also such experts on *human* behavior."

"Sarcasm doesn't suit you, either, Emmie."

"How would you know what suits me?"

"I sure know Ralph Pinstripe doesn't."

"Roger," she corrected wearily.

"I once knew a guy who smiled like that. He's doing time now for trying to fix a race."

"Roger happens to be a highly respected podiatrist."

"No kidding? This guy was in the same line of work. He was a horseshoer."

"Hardly a comparable occupation." Emily reached for the door handle.

"Hold on, Emmie." Chad stilled her with a light touch on her shoulder. "I didn't mean to rile you again. It slipped my mind how high-strung you tend to be. I'm sure Ralph is very good with feet."

Emily took a deep breath. "You didn't *rile* me. I am not *high-strung*. And his name is *Roger.*" Setting him straight for the last time, she hopped out of the Jeep.

"Call me when you decide what to do about Thunder," Chad said in his calm, easygoing manner.

He waved goodbye and drove off, leaving Emily feeling unsettled. She wished he didn't have that effect on her.

Flo called a few days later and invited Emily to have lunch again. She suggested meeting at the Pacific Downs' clubhouse on Saturday.

"Why there?" Emily asked.

"Why not? It seems an appropriate place to discuss Thunderbolt."

What was there left to discuss? Emily wondered. Either Flo was going to buy her share or she wasn't. Coming right out and bluntly stating this, though, seemed rude.

"All right," she agreed. And once she had, she felt good about it. She wanted to see Flo again, for no other reason than that she liked the woman.

Emily spent a long time deciding what to wear for the luncheon Saturday morning. She finally chose a terra-cotta linen jumpsuit, which accentuated her small waist and long legs. She allowed her hair to fall free around her shoulders, a tangle of curls, and took extra time with her makeup.

All the while she dressed Emily pretended that she had no special reason for trying to look her best. But she couldn't block out the image that constantly loomed in the back of her mind—big Chad Barron with his infuriating grin. Not that she expected to see him at the track. He would most likely be spending his time on the back side, not in the clubhouse. Still, there was the vague possibility that they might run into each other. Emily felt silly about the way her stomach fluttered every time she considered this.

Pacific Downs had been built in the twenties and had a certain charm and elegance. The brick grandstand, roofed in slate and supported by white columns, was more reminiscent of Southern rather than Californian architecture. It faced the purpose of its existence—the brown loam track with an infield of emerald green grass.

Huddled just beyond the track were rows of white-washed barns, also roofed in slate, which housed over a thousand racehorses. When Emily stepped out of her economy car in the parking lot, she could smell the presence of these animals and felt an excitement building within her.

The clubhouse was located on the second floor of the grandstand. Following Flo's directions, Emily turned left when she stepped off the escalator and entered the sunny, open dining area. The best tables were those along the long expanse of plate-glass windows, close up to the track action. It didn't surprise Emily to find Flo seated at one of them, dressed in shades of purple again, but with a wide-brimmed hat instead of a turban today. What did surprise Emily was that Flo already had company, a man who looked to be in his sixties, sporting a fifties crew cut.

Flow waved and called loudly when she caught sight of Emily at the entrance. "Come here and meet Sam Seager, sweetie!"

The man stood up as she approached. He was nattily attired in a plaid sports jacket, striped shirt, polka dot bow tie, and checkered slacks. The combination made Emily's head swim.

"It's a pleasure to meetcha," he said, grabbing Emily's hand and pumping it. "From that picture Eddie showed me, I knew you'd grow up to be a long-stemmed American Beauty."

"He had a picture of me?"

"Sure. He used to kiss it for luck before every race."

"Really?" Stunned, Emily could think of nothing else to say.

"Sit down and take a load off your feet," Sam Seager suggested cordially. "We got plenty of time to chat before post time."

Emily sat beside Flo, who patted her arm. "I didn't think you'd mind if I asked Sam to join us. He was with Eddie when he died."

"Yes, my father's landlord told me." She offered Sam a grateful smile. "I was relieved to hear that he had a friend by his side during those last moments, Mr. Seager."

"I want you to know that your father didn't suffer, kid."

"Good," Emily said. That seemed inadequate but she could think of nothing more to add.

"Why'd you go see Eddie's landlord?" Flo asked her.

"I wanted to know what happened to his personal things. Mr. Glick said there was nothing of value and he threw everything out."

"Glick wasn't holding out on you," Sam said. "Your old man didn't have much in the way of worldly goods. A heart of gold, though." He thumped his chest.

The waitress came over and asked if they would like drinks before lunch. She was dressed in a jockey costume but instead of boots she wore very high heels. Flo ordered a Bloody Mary. Sam hesitated until Flo told him that lunch was her treat. Looking relieved, he asked for an imported beer. Emily ordered sparkling water with a lime twist.

"A real yuppie drink," Sam said.

Emily sensed that he meant it as a compliment. She got the feeling that both Sam and Flo held her in high regard simply because she was Eddie Holt's kid.

"What did my father do for a living?" she asked. "His lawyer didn't seem to know much about him."

"Oh, Eddie did this and that to get by," Sam replied vaguely.

"Like what?" Emily pressed.

"Odd jobs here and there. When he made enough money to stake himself, he'd quit and go back to his true vocation."

Emily tensed. "Gambling, you mean? Hardly a productive occupation."

"Eddie liked to think of himself as a professional handicapper," Flo said. "The trouble was he usually ended up betting with his heart instead of his head."

"Yeah, and he lost a lot more than he won," Sam added. "But he kept thinking his luck was about to change. When it did he was going to come back into your life, kid."

"Sure he was." Emily's voice was flat.

"Hey, he thought the world of you," Sam insisted. "He was always bragging about you to us."

Flo patted Emily's arm again. "Didn't I tell you that?"

Emily still found it difficult to believe. "How did he know anything about me? How did he even know I lived in San Francisco? I still don't understand how he was able to give the lawyer my address."

Flo and Sam looked at each other.

"You tell her," Sam said.

"Sweetie, Eddie *followed* you here from Boston when you got transferred."

Emily stared at Flo, trying to make sense of what she had said. "From Boston? He lived there, too?"

"Only because you did," Flo replied. "After you lost your mother Eddie kinda watched over you. It gave him some kind of purpose in life, I suppose."

An overwhelming sadness swept over Emily, and she covered her face with her hands for a moment. When she lowered them her eyes held deep regret. "My God, all those wasted years we could have spent getting to know each other again. Why didn't he ever make his presence known to me?"

Sam cleared his throat. "Eddie didn't want to embarrass you. He was afraid you'd think he was a bum."

"Not that he was one," Flo hurriedly added. "Just a little down on his luck. But Eddie always expected to strike it rich one day. He had all sorts of schemes but he never had the money to fund them. Then one day he finally won big at the track."

"Oh, what a day!" Sam cried. He began talking as if he was experiencing it in the present. "Your old man picks six winners in a row, kid. And for once he leaves the track before he loses it all again. Instead, he hunts down Chad Barron and says he wants to invest in a horse."

"Eddie always knew quality," Flo added. "So naturally he went to the best trainer at Pacific Downs."

"Barron's a shrewd operator, no doubt about it," Sam said. "And he's not afraid to take risks. He's probably the biggest gambler at the track. He stakes his rep on the claimers."

"Thunderbolt was a claimer," Flo said. "Your father had such high hopes for that horse. He was sure Thunder was going to make him a wealthy man."

"And then he was going to get in touch with you," Sam told Emily. "He had this fantasy of picking you up in a limo filled with roses and taking you to the swankiest restaurant in town."

"Eddie had a flair for the dramatic," Flo said with a dreamy little smile. "He reminded me a little of Errol Flynn." Her smile was replaced by a look of concern. "Not that your father was a ladies' man, Emily. I don't want you thinking that."

"Nah, your old man wasn't no skirt chaser, kid," Sam reiterated. "Eddie's passion was the horses."

That gave Emily little comfort. What did comfort her, though, was that her father had loved her from afar. Perhaps he really would have made contact with her if his investment in Thunderbolt had paid off.

"I got something for you," Sam told her.

He shifted in his seat and dug his hand into the back pocket of his checkered slacks. He took out a wallet and handed it across the table to Emily. The brown leather was worn and scarred, ragged around the edges. Emily's heart tightened as she stared at it.

Sam answered the question in her eyes. "Yeah, it belonged to Eddie. I lifted it off him for safekeeping when the ambulance came to take him away. There was twenty-seven bucks in it. Still is. Count it."

"I trust you, Sam," Emily said.

"Look inside," he urged. "At the photo he kept of you."

She opened the wallet with trembling fingers and unsnapped the photo case flap. The plastic windows were yellowed and cracked and empty except for the first one. Enshrined in this window was a snapshot of a little girl on a horse—a carousel horse. Instead of holding on to the rod, she was waving both arms. Her curly head was thrown back and her wide smile revealed missing front teeth. To the side of her, a little out of focus, was a big man with his arm protectively around the girl's waist. Her father. No wonder she had felt so reckless and happy. And so safe.

Emily distinctly remembered the day this picture had been taken by her mother at a county fair. On the way home her parents had argued, which was not unusual. But then her father had stopped the car and stalked off. While her mother drove the rest of the way home, Emily had cried in the back seat, afraid that her father would get lost and not find his way home. How relieved she'd been when he returned to the house later that evening! He'd laughed gently at her concern and promised that he would never be lost to her. But a month or so later he took off for the Saratoga racetrack. And the last communication Emily received from him had been the postcard.

She continued to stare at the photograph now, lost in her private world of memories and oblivious to Sam and Flo. They remained silent until the waitress came with the drinks.

"You get the club soda?" she asked Emily.

Emily looked up with a dazed expression and nodded.

When the drinks were served Flo raised her glass.

"Well, here's to Eddie," she said solemnly.

"Yeah, to Eddie." Sam lifted his beer.

Emily clicked glasses with them, on the verge of bursting into tears. But she held them back, not wanting to make a scene in a public place. Her mother would have been proud of her for showing such self-control. Never once had Emily seen her mother cry over the loss of Eddie Holt.

"Thank you for giving me the wallet," she told Sam.

"Hey, it's rightfully yours, kid. Too bad Eddie's last bet was on that donkey in the fourth or there would have been more money in it. Ah well, you know what they say—you can beat a race, but you can't beat the races." Sam gulped some beer. "Maybe I shoulda had that put on Eddie's tombstone. But I kept things simple. Just his name and the dates."

Emily's throat felt like sandpaper. She took a sip of her soda and barely managed to swallow it. "The lawyer told me that a friend of my father's had arranged his funeral and burial. I appreciate it, Sam. But I wish you had included me."

"I thought about it long and hard," Sam replied. "And I decided that Eddie wouldn't have wanted me to bother you about it."

"Bother me? He was my *father* for goodness' sake!"

"Yeah, well, Eddie felt he'd lost the right to be considered that."

In truth, Emily did, too. But she also felt certain responsibilities and obligations regarding Edmund Holt. "I'll reimburse you," she told Sam.

He shook his head adamantly. "No way, kid. Eddie gave me plenty of hot tips over the years and picking up his last tab was my way of paying him back. Besides, I won big last month and had money to burn."

Emily sensed that she would be insulting Sam if she insisted on reimbursing him. She also sensed that money meant as little to him as it had to Edmund Holt. Her mother had always said that when her father won big, the cash burned a hole in his pocket until he could lose it again.

"Where is my father buried?" she asked Sam softly.

"Not far from here. We used to pass this little cemetery on the way to Pacific Downs every day. It's up on a hill with a great view of the racetrack. Eddie always remarked that he'd like it to be his final resting place."

"God rest his soul," Emily said.

Flo and Sam nodded, and a silence fell over the table for a few minutes.

The waitress broke it by asking them for their lunch orders. Flo insisted that everyone have surf and turf, the most expensive entree on the menu. When it was served Emily stared at the filet mignon and lobster tail on her plate and knew that she would be unable to eat a bite of it.

During the meal Sam pulled out his daily racing form and started discussing the first race with Flo. They went over the horses' past performances and analyzed distance, class, pace and speed factors. Then they assessed the condition of the track, argued over which jockeys were reliable and discussed which trainers had the "winningest" stables.

Intent on their handicapping they didn't notice that they were excluding Emily from their conversation. She didn't mind. In fact she was grateful. She needed time to regain her composure after hearing so many revelations about her father. If only he had made contact with her! Perhaps they could have worked out a relationship. Instead he had left things unsettled between them. She sighed deeply—so deeply that Sam and Flo stopped talking and looked at her.

"Poor Emily, we're boring her," Flo said. "Put away your paper, Sam."

He complied. "Fourth race is the only one I'm betting on today, anyway."

"What's so special about the fourth?" Emily asked him politely although she didn't really care.

Sam looked at Flo. "Didn't you tell her?"

"Not yet. I was saving my surprise for dessert."

"Looks like Em is saving her appetite for dessert, too," Sam observed, giving Emily's untouched food a longing look. "You gonna eat that chunk of meat, kid?"

"No, would you like it?"

"Thanks." He pierced the fillet with his fork and transferred it to his plate before Emily could blink.

"I don't think I want dessert, either," Emily said. "Why don't you tell me what the surprise is now, Flo?" She didn't care for surprises and wanted to get it over with.

"Thunderbolt is entered in the fourth race," Flo announced. "And he stands a good chance of winning."

"No doubt about it," Same said around a mouthful of steak. "Thunderbolt is the only smart bet. When I go to the windows, I'll be happy to place one for you, kid."

"Thank you, I'll pass," Emily said a bit stiffly.

"Never pass up a sure thing," Sam advised.

"Emily has an aversion to gambling," Flo told him. "She thinks it ruined her father."

Same didn't dispute that. Instead he shrugged it off. "I just figured Emily would want to make some money on a horse she's part owner of."

"She doesn't have to bet to do that," Flo said. "All she has to do is keep her fingers crossed."

Emily cleared her throat to remind them that she was still present.

"If Thunder wins, you'll get twenty per cent of the twelve-thousand-dollar purse," Flo told her. "Maybe then you won't be in such a hurry to sell your share."

Sam stopped chewing and looked at Emily, shocked. "You wanna *sell?*"

"I'm not so sure I do anymore," Emily replied. She fingered the leather wallet in her lap, rubbing her thumb along the rough, worn edges.

Her change of heart had nothing to do with the possibility of winning a purse. She knew now that her father hadn't deserted her completely. She was thankful that Flo was giving her a chance to reconsider.

"Why don't we go down to the paddock and visit Thunder before he races?" Flo suggested.

"Count me out," Sam said. "Horses make me nervous up close."

"Will Chad Barron be there?" Emily asked, keeping her tone casual.

"I'd be surprised if he wasn't," Flo replied.

Emily tried to ignore the way her heart began to beat faster. "Yes, I'd like to see Thunderbolt again," she finally said.

Chapter Four

Chad spoke softly to Thunderbolt as he saddled him in the paddock stall. He felt his horses deserved a little personal encouragement from him before they went out to compete. Not that Chad was sentimental about his stock. Horse racing was too tough a business for sentimentality. But he couldn't see the harm in a few kind words and pats, either.

A groom held Thunderbolt's bridle as Chad covered him with a saddle cloth bearing his post position number. He put a sheepskin pad over the cloth to cushion the saddle. A valet, dressed in an official track uniform, placed the properly weighted saddle high on the horse's withers, then passed the girth straps under his belly to Chad. One of them went completely over the top of the saddle to ensure it wouldn't slip during the race. After carefully securing the straps, Chad crouched down and stretched the horse's forelegs to make sure the elastic cinches weren't pinching any skin or muscle. Satisfied, he stood up and stroked Thunderbolt's neck.

"You gonna do me proud today, boy?" he asked.

Thunderbolt's ears pricked forward, a good sign. Then he pawed the ground with his front hooves, an even better sign. Chad interpreted them to mean he was eager to run.

His foreman, Moss, slouched into the stall, his demeanor glum as usual. "Thunder better not act up at the gate again," he grumbled.

Chad wished Moss could be a little more optimistic. Horses picked up on moods. But he remained silent. Old Moss had been with Chad from the start, leaving a cushy job at Sunny Hill Farm to stick with him instead of his father, and Chad would always be appreciative of that. So no matter how churlish he tended to be, Chad tolerated it.

Moss spat out a wad of chewing tobacco and it landed a good ten feet away. "We got visitors, Chad. Couple *investors.*" He spat out that word with the same force. "They wanna wish Thunder luck."

Chad groaned. "Those two are getting to be pests. Remind me not to let any more psychiatrists or car salesmen buy shares in my horses."

"Those two jokers ain't here today," Moss said. "I was referring to the other two. The purple lady and that curly haired gal."

Chad's expression brightened considerably. "Flo Feducci and Emily Holt?"

Moss nodded. "Waitin' by the paddock entrance."

Chad hadn't expected Emily to show up for Thunder's race. He found it even more surprising that he was so pleased that she had, since he usually disliked prerace visits from investors. "Well, bring them back here, Moss. They've got a right to wish their horse luck."

Grumbling to himself, the old man left to do Chad's bidding and returned with the two women. The moment Emily entered the stall Thunderbolt nodded vigorously and released a low-pitched, pulsating sound. Emily stepped back, looking alarmed.

"He's just saying hello," Chad told her. "He must remember you from your visit to my barn."

Emily smiled, looking more amazed than alarmed now, and Chad was glad he had stretched the truth a bit. It was more likely that Thunder had nickered out of simple good spirits than recognition. But Chad was willing to stretch the truth all the way to the half-mile pole to get a smile out of Emily. He thought that she was far too serious most of the time.

"Thunderbolt looks even more beautiful to me than the last time I saw him," she remarked, beaming her smile in Chad's direction.

"I could say the same about you," he replied.

Emily quickly looked away from him. "You're such a tease," she muttered.

Chad hadn't been teasing, but he let it go. No sense arguing over a compliment. He turned his attention to Flo. "Nice of you to come by," he said.

Flo laughed at that. "No need to be polite, Barron. I know you don't appreciate being bothered by your partners before a race."

"Depends on who they are," he replied. "You never cause me any grief, Flo. Where've you been hiding yourself lately?"

"I've been traveling here and there. But I'm back in town for the season." Flo adjusted her big lavender hat. "So level with me, Chadwick. What are Thunder's chances today?"

Chad shrugged. "Just check out the odds on the tote board."

"Forget the board. I want it straight from the horse trainer's mouth."

"Flo darlin', I don't have a crystal ball. Thunder is sound enough, but he's got an unpredictable disposition. And he learned some mighty bad habits before I claimed him."

"Well, he's the favorite in this race," Flo said.

Moss shuffled forward. "Since it's a maiden, that's a vote of confidence for the trainer, not the horse."

"Could also be a vote of confidence for the jockey," Chad pointed out.

Moss snorted. "Ain't hardly likely."

"Jessup's a damn good jock," Chad said, showing rare irritation with Moss.

"For a *female* maybe," the old man allowed.

Emily looked at Chad. "A woman is riding Thunderbolt today?"

He nodded. "Jenny Jessup. One of the most underrated jockeys at the track."

"Then how come you're just about the only trainer willing to give her mounts?" Moss asked.

"Because I know talent when I see it."

Moss shook his head. "Most of the time you do, Chad. But when it comes to this here particular jockey you—"

"Hey, I know what I'm doing and so does she," Chad interrupted. "Subject closed." He didn't mind Moss objecting to his decisions in private, but couldn't abide it in front of investors. Without another word he headed for the walking ring. Moss and the groom, leading Thunderbolt, followed him.

"Come on, Emily," Flo said, hooking arms with her. "We're part of the Barron entourage today."

Emily went along although she didn't care to be part of anyone's entourage, especially one led by Chad "Subject Closed" Barron. She hadn't liked the sharp way he'd spoken to Moss. Not that Moss needed her sympathy. Emily could tell that he was a tough old buzzard. Still, Chad's high-handedness rubbed her the wrong way.

The ring area teemed with action as horses, trainers, owners and grooms joined the eight jockeys dressed in bright silks as they waited for their mounts. Spectators watched from the tiered railings. Some of them made notations in their programs after observing the Thoroughbreds' behavior in the ring.

A jockey slightly taller and far more graceful than the rest waved to Chad. She was wearing a shirt boldly striped in crimson and teal, a crimson helmet, and white breeches that flattered her lean curves. She tapped a whip against her thigh as she approached.

"I always like the way you look in my colors, Jenny," Chad said, greeting her with a broad smile.

"You don't look half-bad yourself today, Chad," she replied and slid her hand down the lapel of his buckskin jacket. Her sharp blue eyes quickly scanned Emily. "I don't believe we've met," she said.

Chad introduced them, explaining to Jenny how Emily had come to own a share of Thunderbolt.

"Welcome to the crazy world of racing," Jenny said. "I promise to do my best for you today, Emily. My best for Thunder, too."

They shook hands. Feeling the strength in Jenny's grip, Emily sensed her strength of character, too, and trusted her to handle Thunderbolt with the highest professionalism.

"Got any last-minute instructions for me?' Jenny asked Chad.

"A few." He wrapped his arm around her shoulder and guided her to a more private area of the ring.

Emily observed them as they talked—Chad hunched over a little to accommodate Jenny's lack of height, Jenny's face turned up to him, her expression earnest. Amidst the commotion around them, they seemed to be encased in an intimate bubble of mutual understanding. What a perfect couple they made, Emily thought, unconsciously biting her bottom lip.

"That little gal's got Chad wrapped around her pinkie," Moss grumbled, also observing them.

"Don't be a prejudiced old coot," Flo said. "He gives Jenny mounts because she gets the job done. Besides, no woman could wrap Chad Barron around her finger."

"He's got a soft spot in his heart for females that can ride good," Moss insisted.

Well, that leaves me out, Emily thought. And then she reminded herself that she wasn't even in the race. Sure, she found Chad physically attractive. Most women would. But as far as she was concerned his obvious sex appeal was more a detriment than an asset. She certainly wanted more than sex in a relationship. She wanted stability. She wanted security. She wanted shared values and interests. The list of what Emily wanted in a man was very long and sensible, and sex appeal wasn't even on it. She wasn't going to make the same mistake her poor mother had.

She looked away from Chad and Jenny, still huddled together, and concentrated on Thunderbolt. Now here was a creature she could admire for his looks alone. His distinctive blaze looked silvery in the sunlight. His coat glowed like polished ebony. His muscles rippled. He was surely the finest-looking horse at Pacific Downs. She glanced around at the others in the ring. None could hold a candle to him. Then her glance snagged on Chad again. His hair glowed like polished ebony. His muscles . . .

"Yoo-hoo, Emily, are you still on this planet?" Flo asked, breaking into her reverie.

Emily forced herself to look away from Chad. "What did you say, Flo?"

"Oh, it doesn't matter. I was just making small talk."

"Sorry I wasn't listening. All this activity distracted me," Emily apologized. "I'm surprised the horses are so calm."

"Most ain't," Moss said. "Take that bay filly swishing her tail back and forth, for instance. See how washy she is?"

"Thunder seems relaxed enough," Emily remarked, observing the horse's cool dignity.

"That's cuz he's a tricky feller," Moss told her. "Sometimes he's on his best behavior and sometimes he acts wild and crazy."

Emily found that difficult to believe until she looked into Thunderbolt's dark wide-set eyes. Beneath their tranquil, luminous surface she could discern an unpredictable wildness. In a flash she saw that he had been trained but not tamed. No one could ever rule Thunderbolt's spirit, she realized. No one could ever destroy it.

Emily smiled at the horse, appreciating for the first time what a magical gift her father had left her. Thunderbolt was her only connection with him now. She felt a deep sadness for Edmund Holt that replaced much of the anger.

The sound of a bugle pierced her thoughts. "Riders up," a paddock official called.

Chad returned with Jenny and boosted her onto Thunderbolt's back. Perched atop the horse, knees high around his neck because of the short stirrups, she gave a confident wave of her whip. The bugle sounded again and a young man on a pony came along and led them away. It happened so quickly that Emily didn't have a chance to give the horse a pat for good luck.

"Where are they going?" she asked Chad.

"To the track. It's time for the post parade. Let's watch it from my box, ladies," Chad suggested.

He escorted Emily and Flo back to the clubhouse. Emily was pleased to see that they had the box all to themselves. There were people seated on either side of them, in other choice seats reserved for owners and trainers, and Chad nodded to them. Emily noted that he didn't go out of his way to be too friendly, but he wasn't aloof, either. He had an aura of self-containment that people seemed to respect.

"I can only stay for this race," he said, sitting down between Emily and Flo. "Then I have to go back to the paddock."

"Why's that?" Emily asked, trying to sound casual rather than disappointed.

"I've got another horse entered in the seventh."

"Boy Wonder," Flo said. She punched Chad's arm. Hard. "That's for not asking me to invest in him, Chadwick."

"I didn't ask anybody, ma'am," Chad replied politely, ignoring the punch. "I own one hundred per cent of Boy Wonder. I didn't acquire him through a claimer of an auction. I bred him. That colt is like kin to me."

"Well, he's a champion, no doubt about it," Flo said.

Chad smiled with pride. "I expect he'll do well in the Pacific Downs Handicap coming up. That purse will make this one seem like small change."

"Track talk is that you're grooming Boy Wonder for the Triple Crown."

"Talk's cheap," Chad replied. "But one thing's for sure. He's the best I got in my barn right now."

Emily wished he would stop talking about how great this Boy Wonder was. What about *her* horse?

She watched Thunderbolt being led past the stands. There were seven other horses in the parade, and seven other ponies to lead them, with red-jacketed outriders to the front and rear. The jockeys' bright silks and white breeches blazed in the sun, the horses' coats gleamed, but this pageantry didn't distract Emily. She only had eyes for one sleek black colt.

"Thunderbolt is the most handsome horse out there," she declared.

Chad grinned. "Not that you're prejudiced or anything."

"Well, he is," Emily insisted. She looked at Chad with an earnest expression. "Don't you agree?"

"This isn't a beauty contest," he replied.

"But Thunder would win hands down if it was," Flo assured Emily in a kindly tone.

This appeased Emily somewhat although she would have appreciated a little praise from the trainer.

"A minute to post time," the track announcer informed the crowd.

A diesel tractor towed the long, partitioned starting gate into position, and then the horses were brought to it.

"They're at the post!" the announcer boomed when they were all behind the gate. The assistant starters, dressed in gray coveralls, began to guide the runners into the narrow stalls.

Emily noticed that Chad's facial muscles had tensed, and she automatically tensed, too, although she didn't know why. "Is something wrong?" she asked him.

"Not yet," he replied, his gaze never leaving the gate.

Most horses entered the stalls willingly or with only a little urging on the part of the starters. Thunderbolt was the last to be loaded and balked when his turn came, digging his hooves into the dirt. Emily heard Chad swear softly under his breath.

"Well, who can blame him for not wanting to go into that tiny space," Emily said in Thunderbolt's defense.

"The point is he has to," Chad said evenly. "That's the way this game is played."

But Thunderbolt wasn't budging. "Maybe you should go out there and encourage him," Emily suggested.

Chad laughed hollowly. "It's out of my hands now, Emmie. Either he'll go in or get scratched."

Emily held her breath as one starter pulled Thunderbolt forward by his bridle and another unceremoniously pushed him into the stall from behind. Jenny remained dignified atop the horse, looking straight ahead. The rear gate slammed shut after Thunderbolt was loaded and Emily exhaled, relieved.

A moment later a bell rang, and the eight front gates flew open simultaneously. The horses exploded onto the track. Emily gasped, caught up in the excitement, and spontaneously reached for Chad's hand. The galloping horses seemed to be one moving mass to her at first and then they became distinct, separate bodies, some angling toward the rail, some falling behind. They moved past her in a blur, though, and she couldn't spot Thunderbolt.

"Where is he? Where is he?" she shrieked, squeezing Chad's big hand with all her might.

"He's still in the gate," Chad replied calmly.

"What?" Emily stared blankly at the track, not understanding, deaf to the announcer and blind to the action. And then it sank in. Thunderbolt wasn't participating in the race. When she finally comprehended this, it was already over.

"What happened?" she asked Chad.

He slowly extracted his hand from her vicelike grip and flexed his fingers a few times as if to make sure they still worked. "What happened?" he repeated, then lifted his shoulders. "He must have froze."

"Do you think he's all right?"

"Why shouldn't he be all right? He sure as hell didn't exert himself today." Chad didn't sound upset about it though. In fact, he seemed completely resigned.

Emily remained concerned. "The people who bet on Thunderbolt will get their money back I hope."

"No way," Flo spoke up. "When a horse refuses to break that's the bettor's tough luck. That's why they're all booing now."

Emily could hear the disgruntled sounds rising from the stands. The people in the surrounding boxes were less vocal, but Emily heard mutterings about Thunderbolt being a deadbeat, a refuser, a bum. First she experienced indignation and then dejection. They were disparaging her beautiful horse.

"Poor Thunder," she said.

"Save your sympathy for his trainer, honey," Chad suggested lightly. "I'm the one who's gonna take flak for this, not that no-account colt."

"Don't you start calling him names, too," Emily pleaded.

Chad slowly shook his head. "Funny, but I can't think of one good thing to say about him at the moment."

"Win some, lose some," Flo put in. "But it would have been nice for Emily to see Thunderbolt actually *run.*"

"Apparently he wasn't in the mood," Chad replied. "Seems he lacks a basic understanding of what a racehorse is expected to do."

"Perhaps he wasn't feeling well," Emily said lamely.

"Thunder's as healthy as a horse," Chad stated.

Flo laughed, but Emily didn't. "I can't understand how you can treat this as a joke," she muttered.

"You either laugh or you cry," Chad told her. "It's just another day at the races."

"It was a little more than that to me," she said wistfully.

Chad swiveled in his seat to look her full in the face. "I'm sorry we couldn't pull off a win for you today, Emily. I would have liked giving you that thrill."

His dark eyes held hers, and she couldn't help wondering what other thrills he could give her. As disappointed as she was about the race, she still managed to notice how thick and spiky his lashes were. And that his eyes weren't black, as she'd supposed, but a deep indigo blue.

"Well, maybe next time," she said a bit breathlessly.

"Next time?" He looked surprised. "You mean you're going to give Thunder another chance?"

Emily nodded.

"But why?" Chad asked. "You were all fired up to sell out a few days ago. I'd think you would be more determined than ever after today's fiasco."

"I can't sell out my father's dream," she said. And something inside her eased up—a coil that had been twisted tight in her chest ever since she'd learned of his death.

"Good for you, partner!" Flo said. "We'll get to the winner's circle with Thunderbolt yet."

Chad didn't look as pleased. "Just don't go falling in love with that horse," he cautioned Emily. "Don't go pinning all *your* dreams on him." He stood up abruptly. "Excuse me, ladies. I have to go see about Boy Wonder."

"What about Thunder?" Emily reminded him. "Shouldn't you see how he's doing, too?"

"Moss is handling him now."

Chad's tone gave Emily the impression that he had more important things to do than deal with a loser. "Thunder won't be . . . disciplined for not leaving the gate, will he?"

"You mean punished?" Chad smiled at Emily. "Of course not, honey. But I reckon all those fans who bet on him would like to see him drawn and quartered on the infield right now." He paused. "Along with his trainer."

"If anyone can get Thunder back on track, you can, Chadwick," Flo said. "I'm willing to give him a little more time with you before I throw in the towel."

Throw in the towel? Emily didn't like hearing that kind of talk now that she had committed herself to Thunderbolt. "Maybe he needs special attention," she suggested to Chad.

"I hear that from every partner about every horse." He glanced at his watch. "I'll come back and watch the seventh race with you," he promised and left the box.

Emily had little interest in the races that followed. She listened politely as Flo filled her in on the action, but her thoughts remained with Thunderbolt. Did horses know when they made a bad showing? she wondered. Did the stable hands treat them with disdain if they did? She hoped Thunder was being treated well now.

"Could we go to Chad's barn and see our horse?" she finally asked Flo, shifting restlessly in her seat.

"Sure. But he's probably being cooled out now. Let's wait awhile longer. We don't want to miss Boy Wonder's performance."

Emily didn't care a hoot about Boy Wonder. Not that she wished him ill. She hoped he would win for Chad's sake. "Is Jenny Jessup the jockey again?" she asked.

Flo checked her form. "No, Willie Budenberry is riding Boy. He's one of the best jockeys on the west coast. A top money winner for over ten years."

"Really?" Emily raised her chin. "Maybe Thunder would have done better if such an experienced jockey had been riding him."

"Maybe," Flo allowed. "Then again, maybe it wouldn't have made the slightest bit of difference. Chad knows a heck of a lot more about matching up horses and jockeys than we do, Emily."

"What about Moss?" Emily countered. "He must know plenty. Chad practically bit off his head when he objected to Jenny."

"Moss shouldn't have argued with him in front of us. Trainers are always concerned about losing face."

"Concerned about losing a very attractive female jockey, too," Emily couldn't help but remark.

"Oh, don't listen to track gossip," Flo said, waving it away with her hand.

But Emily wouldn't let it go. "You mean it's not only Moss who thinks they're involved?"

"Listen, Emily, the backstretch is one of the last male bastions," Flo explained. "So when a trainer gives a pretty jockey a shot, of course rumors circulate that they're sleeping together. Personally, I don't believe Chad operates that way. I can't imagine a good-looking man like that having to *bribe* a woman to go to bed with him."

Neither could Emily. "But what if Jenny's in love with him and the feeling is mutual?" she asked Flo. "Wouldn't that cloud Chad's judgment about her skills as a jockey?"

"Shh," Flo hissed, giving her a poke.

Emily glanced around to see Chad coming down the aisle. He took the seat between them again.

"Were you talking about me?" he asked Flo nonchalantly. "I saw you give Emmie a poke when you spotted me."

"Actually, we were discussing your love life," Emily said, surprising herself by admitting it.

Chad laughed it off, assuming she was joking. He pointed out Boy Wonder in the post parade. Flo expressed her admiration again but Emily remained silent. The gray colt didn't look the least bit extraordinary to her. Not compared to Thunderbolt, anyway.

"Five minutes to post time," the track announcer advised over the intercom.

Flo leaped up. "I want to place a bet on Boy Wonder. If I can't make it back here in time I'll watch the race from the lounge. Good luck, Chadwick." She hustled off to the betting windows, leaving Chad and Emily alone.

"Jenny sends her condolences," he said.

"How kind." Emily's voice was flat.

"There was nothing she could do, you know. It's up to the horse in the end."

Emily remained doubtful. "You're using a different jockey for Wonder Boy," she said.

"Boy Wonder," he corrected. "Yes, I am. So?"

"I'd just like to know why."

"Lots of reasons." But Chad didn't proceed to tell her what they were.

"I hear Budenberry is an excellent jockey. Nothing but the best for your precious Boy." Emily smiled, hoping it would make her comment less caustic.

Chad didn't smile back. "I don't play favorites, Emmie. I want every horse I train to win, and I choose riders that suit them. Thunder performs best with gentle encouragement, which he gets from Jenny. She relies on her voice and touch, not the whip."

Emily could hardly object to that. "Then why didn't you have her ride Boy as well?"

"Maybe next time I will. But today I chose Willie to get the job done."

"Why?" Emily persisted.

"Because he's more familiar with Boy and with the other competitors in this particular race," Chad explained with a great show of patience.

"And this race is more important to you than Thunder's was," Emily said.

"Yes, it is," Chad admitted without hesitation. "The purse is a lot bigger, and I don't have to split it with any partners. But that has nothing to do with my choice of jockeys."

"Hah! Tell me another one."

"I will tell you one more thing." Chad leaned close to her so that she would hear every word. He kept his voice low, and she could feel his warm breath on her neck as he spoke. "I don't appreciate having some greenhorn like you trying to second guess my motives or decisions. You don't know diddly-squat about this business, and I've been in it all my life."

Emily shifted uncomfortably after being put in her place. But she had to admit that he was right. She didn't know enough about horse racing to question his decisions, let alone argue with him about them. She resolved there and then to learn all she could about it as quickly as possible.

"Enough said." Satisfied that he'd made his point, Chad leaned back and took her in with an all-encompassing glance. "I like that thing you've got on, Emmie."

"Thing?" Caught off guard by the sudden turn in conversation, Emily looked down at her own person.

"That outfit of yours," he said. "I don't know what it's called."

"A jumpsuit," she told him.

"A jumpsuit?" he repeated, grinning. "Are you a parachutist in your spare time?"

She laughed. "Hardly!"

"So what *do* you do in your spare time?"

Emily wondered if he was trying to get to know her better or just get her off the subject of jockeys. Whatever his motive, she wished she could give him a fascinating answer. But she couldn't. Her life was too tame.

"Oh, I read a lot," she said. "I like to rummage through junk shops and second-hand book stores." Lord, how dull can you get? she thought. She held back that she collected salt and pepper shakers, afraid that he would start nodding off.

"Do any sports?" he asked her.

"No, not since high school." She didn't want to talk about that. "What interests you when you're not working, Chad?"

"My work is my life right now," he said. "When I'm not training horses I'm breeding them. I own a small ranch about thirty miles from here. Nothing fancy. But a start."

"A start to what end?"

"I intend to be the best Thoroughbred breeder in the country some day."

"Just this country?" Emily asked archly. "What about the entire world?"

Chad nodded. "That, too." He was dead serious.

"You think big."

"I was raised to."

"I was raised to think small," Emily told him. "My mother thought that would save me from future disappointments." She paused. "And it has," she added.

"Well, you were sure disappointed today," Chad reminded her. "I'm not going to make excuses for Thunder's bad show, Emmie. The buck stops here." He jabbed his chest with his thumb.

"I don't want excuses. But I'd like an explanation," she said. "Why was he the only horse that refused to run?"

Chad hesitated. "If I told you it would sound like I was *passing* the buck."

"Tell me anyway."

"All right. I suppose you have a right to know. Thunder had a rough time of it before I claimed him. Bad enough that his previous trainer was incompetent, but he was downright mean to boot. I've witnessed that son of a gun break many a good horse's spirit."

"But not Thunderbolt's!" Emily objected. "He has plenty of spirit."

Chad looked surprised. "What makes you so sure?"

"I saw it in his eyes." Emily laughed nervously. "Does that sound dumb?"

"No. Not at all. You can see it in people's eyes, too." Chad studied her with interest. "No one could ever break your spirit, Emmie."

He was right about that, Emily thought. She'd had plenty of setbacks in life, but she'd never been down for long. Still, she self-consciously lowered her eyes from his scrutiny.

"And you're right about Thunderbolt," he continued without missing a beat. "He still has grit. But he lacks motivation. Trouble is, Thunder is well on his way to developing a mighty fractious disposition. The way I figure it, he can't see any advantage in racing since he wasn't properly rewarded for his effort in the past."

"You can change his attitude, can't you?" Emily asked hopefully.

"I wouldn't have claimed him if I didn't think I could."

This made Emily feel a lot better. At that moment she trusted Chad. "Will you give Thunderbolt special attention?" she asked, sounding more like a concerned mother than a disinterested investor.

"As much as I can," Chad replied. "But every horse in my barn needs attention."

None was more deserving than *her* horse, Emily thought. She couldn't come right out and say that, though.

Chad dropped the subject and watched as Boy Wonder was loaded into the starting gate. Unlike recalcitrant Thunderbolt, he pranced into his assigned slot without giving the assistant starter a moment's trouble. When the bell rang he broke out of the gate ahead of the pack and stayed in the lead, unchallenged, throughout the race. Chad remained calm, almost indifferent as he watched. Only when Boy Wonder crossed the finish line did he show any emotion. Cheering, he rose to his feet, then plucked Emily up as if she were a flower. "What'd you think of that, honey?" he asked her, eyes gleaming with pride.

Emily opened her mouth to reply, but it was instantly covered by Chad's. His kiss was swift and hard and took her breath away. Then he softened it, gently molding his wide mouth to her full lips as he slid his hand up her back and under her thick, curly hair. He gently cupped his palm behind her neck, stroking the soft, sensitive skin along the side of her throat with his callused thumb.

The roughness of his touch, combined with the sublime gentleness of his mouth caused Emily to shiver with delight. She allowed him to explore her mouth with his tongue and savor her more intimately. Molded against his big hard body, she felt a sweet melting deep within her. She forgot where she was, who she was, and gave in to the pleasure of this lingering moment. She couldn't have put a stop to it if she'd wanted to, but it didn't even occur to her to stop him.

Chapter Five

It was Chad who broke away. Taking a step back he stared down at Emily, his dark eyes gleaming even brighter than before. He looked disturbed, almost angry. At that moment Flo came bustling down the aisle and joined them.

"Congratulations, Chad!" she cried. "I saw the race from the lounge. Boy Wonder put in a perfect performance."

Chad hesitated for only a fraction of a second, then turned away from Emily. He wrapped his long arms around Flo's rotund figure and gave her a big smack on the cheek.

"Any gal within reach gets a kiss from me when my horse wins," he declared. "It's an old Barron custom."

His disclaimer didn't fool Emily. Maybe Chad had grabbed and kissed her because she happened to be the only female within reach when his horse crossed the finish line. But their embrace had turned into something more than a customary expression of victory. Hadn't it?

Doubt began to gnaw at Emily as Chad discussed the race in detail with Flo. He barely looked her way and when he did his expression was polite but disinterested, as if they hadn't shared anything special a few minutes before. She licked her lips, recalling the feel and taste of his mouth on hers. Had she reacted too strongly? Had it been completely one-sided on her part?

"Come back to my barn for the celebration," Chad told Flo. "Oh, and you too, Emmie," he added, as if he'd just remembered that she still existed.

Emily's immediate inclination was to refuse. But she wanted to check up on Thunderbolt. "Sure, why not?" she said as nonchalantly as she could. Vowing that she would never let Chad know that his kiss had affected her so strongly, she kept her expression blank as she looked directly at him.

Chad did not quite meet her eyes. "Well, let's go," he said brusquely and led the way out of the box.

The party turned out to be an informal gathering in Chad's office. His staff of grooms, handlers, hot walkers and exercise riders partook in the celebration, along with an assortment of backstretch denizens who wandered in. When Willie Budenberry arrived, still dressed in his silks, everyone applauded. Boy Wonder was toasted time and time again, at first with champagne and later with beer, the beverage of choice for most of the back side population.

The camaraderie was strong and so was the language. Flo fit right in but Emily hung back, nursing her plastic cup of champagne as she observed, rather than participated. Mostly she observed Chad.

What made him tick? Emily wondered. Why had he kissed her like that and then ignored her? She wished that she could simply forget about it, as Chad obviously had. He sat in his swivel chair, booted feet propped up on his desk, as his friends and associates paid court to him. Not that Chad acted as if he expected to be courted. There was nothing the least bit imperious about his bearing. At the same time there could be no question that he quietly ruled this backstretch principality of his, maintaining complete control at all times.

Other trainers dropped by to congratulate him on his win, and Emily could see that they held him in high regard, even though they kidded around and pretended they didn't. All the trainers were male, along with most of the employees, except for a few young women who worked as grooms and hot walkers. Flo had been right, Emily decided. The backstretch was a male-dominated world, and women held fairly low positions in the pecking order.

Then Jenny Jessup sauntered in, looking as fresh as dew in a yellow knit top and white jeans. She impatiently tossed back her long mane of blond hair as she strolled through the crowded room. People stepped aside for her. If there was a reigning princess of the back side, Emily thought, it was surely Jenny, the only female jockey at Pacific Downs. She made her way straight to Chad.

"Sorry I couldn't do it for you in the fourth," she told him.

"That's because he saddled you with a donkey, sweetheart," one of the other trainers put in.

"Whoa there, sport," Chad objected over the laughter that followed. "Don't go denigrating one of my horses when you're a guest in my barn. It's downright rude."

But his manner was genial, and Emily felt disappointed that he hadn't defended Thunderbolt more vigorously. It sounded to her as if he were defending some kind of backstretch protocol instead. She waited for either Flo or Jenny to put in a good word for Thunderbolt but neither spoke up.

So Emily felt obliged to. "Thunderbolt is *not* a donkey," she said, tremulous voice raised. "You can tell what a fine racehorse he is just by looking at him."

A silence followed as people turned to stare at her with puzzled looks. Who the heck was she? they seemed to be asking. And why had she said something so utterly stupid?

"One of Thunder's owners," Chad explained to the group in general. "You know how owners are."

That sounded rather condescending to Emily, but his simple explanation seemed to satisfy everyone. They stopped looking at her and continued their chatter and horsing around. Someone passed her a bag of corn chips. To be polite, Emily extracted one but didn't eat it. Her throat was dry enough.

As soon as she was sure no one was looking at her anymore, Emily slipped away from the party and went down the long shed row in search of Thunderbolt. The party chatter dimmed as she strolled farther and farther away. She could still hear the music, though, piped into each stall.

Did racehorses have a good time? Emily wondered. Did they enjoy their exclusive, restricted existence? From what she had observed during her last visit to the backstretch, Emily knew that an inordinate amount of care went into their daily maintenance. Glancing into each stall as she passed, she noticed how neat and clean they were kept. It was clear that Chad Barron's domain was a well-ordered place even though it seemed chaotic at times.

The barn was more peaceful in the late afternoon than in the morning. Horses gazed out at Emily over the scarred Dutch doors, and their earthy scent enveloped her. The elegant beauty of their sleek necks and heads moved Emily almost to tears. There was no doubt about it, she thought, she could easily become an ardent horse lover.

She kept moving slowly up the shed row, searching for the horse she could love most. And when she came to Thunderbolt's stall he nickered again in greeting. Emily released a throaty laugh of pleasure in return.

"You really do recognize me, don't you, Thunder?"

She wished she had something to give him—a carrot or sugar cube or whatever it was horses appreciated as treats. She remembered the corn chip still cupped in her hand. Dare she offer him that? Would he bite off her fingers if she did? She looked him in the eye and could see her reflection in the dark depths. No, she decided, Thunderbolt would never hurt her. Still, her hand shook slightly as she uncurled it in front of his face. The chip lay on the pillow of her palm, her offering to this magical beast.

The way it disappeared seemed also magical—Emily barely felt the touch of Thunderbolt's lips as he daintily plucked it from her hand.

"You're a *wonderful* horse," she told him. "The best in the world. I know you can outrun the wind when you want to. I've seen you do it in my dreams."

"Dreams don't count, Emmie."

Emily whirled around and came face to chest with Chad. As her eyes rose from his chest to his shoulders to his face, Emily remembered that it wasn't quite Thunderbolt she dreamed of, but a centaur whose front half strongly resembled Chad's muscular upper torso. Luckily, dreams could remain private if one didn't care to share them. And Emily had no intention of sharing hers with Chad.

"Why'd you follow me out here?" she asked him.

"I was concerned that you were upset about something."

"Well, I am. I don't like hearing my horse being disparaged."

"Don't take it to heart, honey. The trainer who called him a donkey was just trying to get back at me because I claimed some good horses off him in the past." Chad smiled. "And I'll do it again."

They gazed at Thunderbolt in silence for a moment, standing close together but not touching.

Chad cleared his throat. "Anything else bothering you, Emmie?"

"Yes. The way you..." Emily stopped talking and pushed some straw around with the tip of her shoe.

"The way I what?" he prodded.

Kissed me and then ignored me, she had intended to say. "Patronized me at the party," she said instead.

"Did I?" Chad looked genuinely surprised. "Now how'd I manage to do a thing like that?"

Emily realized that she would sound petty if she told him. "Oh, forget it," she said.

"Okay," he agreed breezily. "Now come back to the party." He took hold of her hand.

She pulled it away. "No, I don't fit in there. I'm not good at mixing with people. I'm sort of a loner."

"Same here," Chad said.

"You?" It was Emily's turn to look surprised. "But you're surrounded by people every day."

"It's horses I surround myself with, Emmie. The people just come with the territory."

Did pretty jockeys also come with the territory? Emily couldn't get up the nerve to ask him that.

"And don't get the wrong idea about us partying it up every time we win a race," Chad continued. "Boy Wonder is a special case."

Here we go again, Emily thought. More accolades for his favorite horse.

"See, my crew gets a bigger bonus than usual when Boy wins," Chad said. "I always give them a percentage of my share of a purse and since I'm sole owner of Boy, I have more to divvy up with them."

"You mean it's just money that motivates everybody's enthusiasm for that horse?"

Chad smiled at her naiveté. "Money is always the main motivation at a racetrack, Emmie. If a horse can't earn his keep he's worthless to us."

Thunderbolt snorted as if to object.

"Listen up, buddy," Chad said, shaking a finger at him. "We got no room for hay burners around here."

His tone was bantering, but Emily sensed that he meant what he said. "You're pretty tough under that easygoing act of yours, aren't you, Chad?"

He laughed. "It's no act. I have a pretty laid-back nature unless I get riled or crossed. But you've got to be tough in this business. The minute you go soft, you go under." He looked at Thunderbolt again. "If need be, you cut your losses."

"But you're dealing with living creatures, not disposable merchandise, Chad."

"I don't let myself get tangled up emotionally with my stock." He paused. "Matter of fact, I don't want to get emotionally involved with anything or any*body* right now. I want you to understand that, Emmie."

Emily nodded, understanding him perfectly. He'd searched her out to tell her this specifically. "Then you'd better tone down your custom of kissing women when your horses win, mister," she replied in a cool voice. "Some might get the wrong idea."

"I hope you didn't. I apologize for getting a little carried away."

Emily forced a laugh. "That's the first time a man's told me he was sorry for kissing me! Forget about it, Chad. I certainly have." She intended to, anyway.

"I just wanted to clear the air."

"Well, you have."

So it was settled, Emily thought. Their kiss would lead to nothing. Not that she'd wanted it to. All the same, she found herself imagining what a racehorse must feel like when it's all primed up and ready to go but gets disqualified right before post time.

"Sure you won't come back to the party?" Chad asked her.

She knew he was only being polite. "No, I really should be heading back to the city. I have to meet someone for dinner."

"That stuffed shirt in the pinstripe suit?"

Emily ignored his teasing reference to Roger. If he didn't want to get personal, he had no right to ask her personal questions. On the other hand, she still had her rights as his partner, and he wasn't going to get rid of her that easily.

"I intend to keep close tabs on Thunderbolt from now on, Chad. I hope you don't mind." She didn't really care if he did.

His expression became more guarded. "I don't mind my partners taking an interest in their investment so long as they don't make a nuisance of themselves."

"What exactly do you consider a nuisance?"

"When they start acting as if they know better than I do."

"Isn't there at least the *possibility* that someone could?"

"Not when it comes to training horses." Chad widened his stance and folded his arms across his chest.

How stubborn he looked, Emily thought. Like a bull. A big burly bull. Well, she could be stubborn herself. "When is Thunderbolt's next race?" she demanded.

"Haven't picked one yet. I'll have to check out the condition book."

"I don't know what that is," Emily said, hating to admit it.

"It's the publication the track puts out listing all the upcoming races and terms for eligibility. I'll enter Thunder in a suitable spot as soon as I can. He sure doesn't need a rest period after today." Chad turned to the horse. "You got a real performance problem, sport. We're going to have to work on it before you compete again."

"Will you keep me apprised of his progress?" Emily asked.

"Apprised?" Chad grinned at her. "Is that how they talk at your fancy accounting office, honey?"

"Will you?" she asked evenly.

"Only if his progress is spectacular. Like if he starts talking or tap dancing or something."

Emily shifted impatiently from one foot to the other. "In other words, you're not going to."

"I don't have the time, Emmie." Chad also shifted impatiently. "Hell, if I had to *apprise* all my partners about all the horses I train, I couldn't get any work done. But I'll call you when Thunder's scheduled to race again, okay?"

She supposed it would have to be okay. "Thank you," she said perfunctorily.

"The least I can do."

"The very least," Emily muttered.

"Hey, we're on the same side," he reminded her. "We both want Thunder to develop into a winner." Chad looked over her shoulder and smiled with satisfaction at what he saw. "Like the horse coming along right now."

Emily turned to see Chad's nephew Bobby Lee leading Boy Wonder up the shed row. The gray colt was covered by a plaid blanket.

"You cool him out good, Bobby?" Chad asked.

"You bet. I personally washed him and then walked him for almost an hour." The young man greeted Emily with a tip of his cap. "I'm the only one Chad trusts to take care of his prize horse,'' he told her. ''Lucky me! Everybody else gets to party.''

''Poor mistreated kid.'' Chad took the horse's lead shank from Bobby. ''Go join the party. I'll do Boy up.''

''Thanks, Chad. You're not such a slave driver after all.'' Pleased to be relieved of his duties, Bobby said goodbye to Emily and hurried off.

''He seems like a nice boy,'' Emily told Chad.

Chad nodded. ''My eldest sister's first born. He dropped out of school back in Louisville and started running with a bad crowd. So I offered to take him in and keep an eye on him.''

''That was a generous thing to do, considering your reluctance to get involved with anybody,'' Emily couldn't help remarking.

''Family's different. Because they're kin, you're automatically involved. I'd do just about anything for my sisters and their brood.''

Chad's declaration of family loyalty soothed Emily's irritation with him. ''Do you have any brothers?''

''Nope. I'm the youngest and only son. My five sisters doted on me, growing up.''

Emily arched a brow. ''Under those conditions, some men would grow up assuming they were God's gift to women.''

''I expect some men would.''

''But not *you*, of course.''

''I'm as unassuming as they come, Emmie.''

They both laughed over that.

''Well, I should be leaving,'' Emily said. She transferred her handbag from one arm to the other, as if that would give her the impetus she needed.

"And I'd better do up Boy before the evening feeding," Chad said. He also stayed where he was.

"What's that mean? Do up?"

"Come back to Boy's stall and I'll show you."

What harm could there be in staying a little while longer? After all, she wanted to learn all she could about the care and training of horses now that she was committed to Thunderbolt. She followed Chad and Boy Wonder down the straw-strewn aisle.

Chad hitched Boy to the back of the stall and removed the horse's blanket. Then he removed his jacket. "Can't get dressed up in this business," he said. "Seems we're always shorthanded, and I fill in as groom as often as not. No sirree, no pinstripe suits for the likes of me."

A little smile played on Emily's lips as she watched Chad roll up the sleeves of his blue denim shirt, exposing his strong, hairy forearms. "A suit wouldn't suit you," she joked.

"The only time I intend to wear one is the day I get married."

"I'm surprised you plan to get married at all. I mean, that does take a certain amount of emotional involvement."

Chad winced. "You going to keep reminding me I said that?"

Emily intended to keep reminding *herself.* "I won't mention it again," she told Chad.

"Good." His dark eyes studied her for a long moment. "I hope you don't make me eat those words someday, Emmie."

His voice was so soft that Emily had to strain to hear him. Even then, she wasn't sure she'd heard correctly. And if she had, what on earth did he mean?

Was he teasing her again? Or coming on to her? Or simply expressing a fear of falling for any woman? Chad gave no clues. He turned his attention to Boy Wonder.

Deciding that she would never understand a man like Chad Barron, Emily leaned against the rough wall and watched him run his hands across the colt's body. "I'm feeling for pain," he said after a few minutes.

"How can you feel pain? It isn't tangible."

"No, but muscles and joints are. And I can feel heat in them if they're sore." Chad continued smoothing his palms along the horse's shoulders, barrel and back. "Since a horse can't tell you what's bothering him, you have to build a relationship based on touch and trust."

"Touch and trust," Emily repeated. If only relationships between men and women could be based on something so pure and simple. "You love your work, don't you, Chad?"

"I don't know if you'd call it love exactly. I'm here sunrise to sundown seven days a week. No vacations. No weekends off. If anyone works like a horse, it's *me,* not my Thoroughbreds." He shook his head. "And you know what, Emmie? I do it because I want to. Does that sound crazy?"

"Not if it makes you happy. Does it?"

"I don't know." He crouched to run his hands up and down Boy's front legs. "All I know is that it's like breathing to me. I can't separate myself from my horses. I find a real peace in that special place I share with them."

As Emily listened to his quietly spoken words, she appreciated the way he expressed himself so simply and naturally. Perhaps she could eventually come to understand a man like Chad Barron after all, she mused. At the same time she felt more alienated from him than ever, sensing that no one got in the special place between him and his animals. No one.

She watched Chad continue to examine the colt from head to hooves. He moved slowly, deliberately, as if he had all the time in the world. Here in the shadowy stall time seemed to stand still. Emily was dimly aware of the music in the background, a female country singer lamenting about how difficult it was to pull back the reins when love overtakes you. Emily paid little attention to it and concentrated on Chad instead. He moved like a man who knew exactly what he was doing. She liked that.

And Chad liked the way she was watching him so closely. There was nothing more satisfying, more warming to the heart and ego, he thought, than a pretty woman watching your every move.

Not that Emmie's avid attention necessarily meant that she was admiring *him*. Chad figured she was so interested in everything he did because of her growing fascination with Thoroughbreds in general and Thunderbolt in particular. He didn't usually like outsiders hanging around his barn. But he didn't mind Emily being here now. He didn't mind at all. She didn't talk too much, a trait he appreciated in a woman. In a man, too.

Chad went to the corner of the stall to get a bucket and brought it over to Emily. ''Care for a facial, pretty lady?''

Emily looked into the bucket and made a face. ''That's mud.''

''Not your run-of-the-mill mud, though. This stuff's special. Comes all the way from Bowie, Maryland. I always do my horses up in Bowie mud after a race.'' Chad knelt in the deep layer of straw lining the stall and began coating Boy's legs with the dark clay.

''That looks like fun,'' Emily said.

''Come on over and try it.''

It was certainly the most unique invitation Emily had ever received from a man. She only hesitated for an instant. In the next she was kneeling beside Chad and sinking her hands into the mud bucket. She laughed with delight.

''Pack it around the fetlock,'' Chad said.

''The what?''

''The ankle. Really spread it thick.'' Chad chuckled softly as she followed his instructions. ''You're not afraid to get your hands dirty, are you, Emmie?''

''No, I like it.''

''Doesn't fit my image of you.''

Emily paused to look at him. ''Really? What sort of image?''

''Oh, I don't know. Kinda prim and proper. Spick-and-span. Miss Perfect.''

Hardly a sexy image, Emily thought as she resumed coating the colt's front leg with mud. ''I suppose I am a bit of a perfectionist,'' she admitted. ''But it's not a bad trait to have when you're an accountant.''

''Did you always want to be a bean counter?''

''Not *always*. I mean, it's not the sort of career a little girl dreams of having.''

''Then what did you dream of becoming?'' Chad asked in a tone that made Emily believe he was truly interested.

Emily didn't answer him, though. ''Why on earth are we doing this?'' she asked instead.

''What? Having a personal conversation?''

"No, plastering Boy's legs with mud."

"Oh, it draws out the heat and soreness. A Thoroughbred's legs take a real pounding during a race. Don't forget, they support over a thousand pounds of weight."

Emily ran her hand up the colt's slender leg, feeling the bone and tendons beneath her palm.

"It's no wonder they're always breaking down," Chad continued. "Frankly, I don't think that racing is any more natural for horses than the hundred-yard dash is for men."

Emily's heart jumped. "Or for women."

"Women sprinters?" Chad shrugged. "Don't know any."

"You do now, mister."

"You?" Chad stopped working on the horse and gave her his full attention. "You're a runner, Emmie?"

"Was. Past tense. We're talking ancient history."

"Heck, you're not that old. How ancient?"

"High school. During my senior year I won the women's state championship in the hundred-yard dash."

"Well, I'll be damned!" Chad sat back on his haunches and continued to stare at her. "I'm mighty impressed, Emmie."

Although she hadn't intended to tell him about her own racing days, the glow of his approval warmed her and she opened up like a flower. "A coach from Boston University was assigned to work with me after that. To get me ready for the Olympics."

"You were in the Olympics?" Chad's admiring look turned to one of amazement.

Emily shook her head. "No, I never made it. My knee gave out. Torn cartilage. They call it a deranged knee." She laughed. "*I* was the one who felt deranged after wearing a cast for six months."

"Poor kid." Forgetting his hand was muddy, Chad patted her back, leaving his imprint on her. Neither of them noticed. "Didn't you go back into training after your knee healed?"

"No. There was a big change in my life and I gave up running. I lost interest in it."

"What sort of change?"

She didn't want to talk about her mother's fatal car accident. "Oh...other things became more important. Like getting a degree. I put myself through college on a work scholarship and didn't have time to train anymore."

"So you gave up your dream."

"I outgrew it. I had to consider the future and how I would support myself. There aren't many job openings for sprinters, you know." Emily paused and looked up at Boy Wonder. "Except if you're a horse, of course." She managed a smile.

And Chad's heart turned over.

Chapter Six

Fighting back the temptation to take her into his arms, Chad straightened abruptly and went to the side of the stall for some brown paper bags, which he began tearing into strips. He concentrated intensely on this simple task. He had no intention of letting Emily Holt get to him. He wasn't going to let a brave little smile and a pair of dreamy golden eyes turn him into mush.

The moment Chad left her side Emily felt cold. It was his silent rebuff that chilled her. He'd obviously lost interest or grown impatient with her personal history. He had no time for bad-luck stories. All he cared about was winners.

"Hey, Chad?" Jenny Jessup leaned over the stall door. "Aren't you coming back to the party?" Then she noticed Emily kneeling in the hay. "You're going to get that pretty outfit of yours all dirty," she warned. But her smile was friendly enough.

"Emmie wanted to watch how we do up a horse," Chad explained.

He returned to her side with the brown paper strips and proceeded to wrap them around the colt's mudded ankles. Since he didn't ask Emily to help him, she rose to her feet and held her mud encased hands awkwardly away from her body.

Jenny laughed at her predicament. "Looks like you were doing more than watching, Emily. Lucky thing you don't have an itch to scratch." An expert on timing because of her trade, Jenny waited a beat. "Or do you?" She tilted her head, ever so slightly, in Chad's direction.

"No, I don't have an itch," Emily said and instantly disliked how prim she had sounded. She attempted a lighter tone. "But I *do* have to drive home now. Is there anywhere I can rinse this gunk off?"

"Sure there is. I'll show you where," Jenny offered.

"Could you carry my handbag out for me?" Emily pointed to it in the hay and Jenny plucked it up.

Emily turned to Chad, who was now intent on wrapping white bandages over the brown paper as Boy Wonder patiently tolerated the procedure. "Well, so long," she said, waving her muddy hand.

Chad looked up, as if surprised she still existed. "Yep. See you around, Emmie. Take care now."

And that was it. He went back to his task. Having been dismissed so succinctly, Emily left the stall and followed Jenny down the shed row. When Thunderbolt saw them approaching he nickered.

"He's asking for a treat, the no-good beggar," Jenny said. She gave him a playful brush on the nose. "You let me down real good today, Thunder."

"Has that ever happened to you before?" Emily asked. "A horse refusing to leave the gate?"

The friendliness in Jenny's eyes diminished considerably. "What do you mean by that?"

Emily raised her shoulders. What else could she mean except exactly what she'd asked?

"Listen, it's not *my* fault your horse refused to run today," Jenny told her. "Sometimes you can whip a horse into cooperating but I was sure Thunder would buck if I did. It's a dangerous thing to do when you're in a tight spot like a gate stall. The horse can injure himself, or the assistant starter, or throw you."

"Oh, I wasn't suggesting you should have whipped Thunder!" Emily protested.

"Then what were you suggesting?"

"Nothing." Emily gave Jenny a direct look. "Can't I ask a simple question?"

A long moment passed before Jenny replied. "Sure you can, Em. Sorry if I seem edgy. But I don't like to lose a race like that, without even getting a chance to run it."

"I'm sorry about that, too," Emily said.

"Oh well." Jenny nudged Thunderbolt's nose again. "No hard feelings."

She was talking to the horse, but Emily guessed that she was really addressing her. They continued down the shed row together.

"What made you become a jockey?" Emily asked.

"Chad."

"Oh." Emily's heart dipped. "I should have guessed."

"Yeah, I started out as his gallop girl."

"His what?"

"An exercise rider," Jenny explained. "Chad spotted my talent and encouraged me to get a jockey's license. I was eighteen at the time, and I've been with him ever since."

As a jockey or lover? Emily wished she had the nerve to inquire. "Then you and Chad go back a long way," she commented instead.

"Hey, I'm not that old!" Jenny laughed. "But we do go back a ways. Nearly seven years. Chad was just starting out at Pacific Downs himself when we met. He was in his early twenties and determined to make it as a trainer. He staked himself with a few horses he managed to claim cheap. But he didn't treat them cheap, if you know what I mean."

Emily nodded. "He gave them the care and training and respect you would a champion."

"Right." Jenny looked at Emily as if she wasn't so dumb after all. "Some of the other trainers grouse that Chad was just born lucky. But that's sour grapes. The secret to Chad's success is hard work and dedication."

Emily smiled her approval. She valued such traits.

"He's also the biggest gambler around here," Jenny added.

Emily's smile faded. "You mean Chad bets heavily on the horses?"

"Not at the windows," Jenny said. "He stays clear of that. But claiming is the poker of the backstretch and Chad Barron plays for high stakes. He likes to claim unproven horses like Thunderbolt." Jenny sighed. "Sometimes that doesn't work out so great."

"You don't think Thunderbolt will work out?" Emily waited apprehensively for Jenny's answer.

But Jenny avoided a direct reply to her question. "Thoroughbreds are full of surprises. Heck, that's what makes horse racing." She turned on a spigot at the side of the barn. "Here, help yourself, Em."

As Emily rinsed the mud off her hands under the tap she could feel Jenny's eyes on her. But when she looked up Jenny glanced away. "Sure is a pretty sunset this evening," the jockey said, looking at the sky.

Sunset? Emily hadn't noticed the changing light. She turned off the spigot and checked her watch. "Oh, no," she said. "I have a dinner date in less than half an hour. I didn't realize it was getting so late."

"Time tends to slip away when you're in good company." Jenny gave Emily a knowing smile. "And he *is* good company, isn't he?" With that, she handed Emily her bag, turned on her heel and headed back down the shed row without bothering to say goodbye.

Habitués of the back side, Emily decided, didn't waste much time with formalities. Flapping her hands in the air to dry them, she hurried to the parking lot. She hoped the traffic would be light driving back to the city. She was meeting Roger Molby at a restaurant downtown, and he was a stickler for punctuality.

Chad had finished wrapping Boy's legs, but he stayed in the stable, reluctant to return to the party. He wanted a little time alone.

He thought about Emmie being a champion runner and smiled. He could always spot winners, and he'd given her high marks when he'd checked out her coltish legs the first time they'd met. He recalled how he'd had such mixed feelings about her. Naturally he'd been attracted to her. She was a good-looking woman.

He'd found her cool manner off-putting, though. Her tough attitude regarding her father's legacy belied the tenderness he'd seen in her soft golden eyes. It hadn't seemed quite fair to Chad that she could look so inviting and act so remote. He remembered how relieved he had felt when she'd left his barn that morning. Hadn't he told himself it would be best if he never saw her again?

Then why in blazes had he gone out of his way to stop by her office a few days later? Well, that was just business. Like hell it was, Chad muttered. He'd gone to get a second look. He'd wanted to see if Emily Holt's eyes were as golden as he'd remembered them and her legs as shapely. They had been.

So he'd helped her out a little by taking her to her father's boarding house. It could have ended there, no harm done. They could have remained friends, occasionally bumping into each other at the track. But then he'd taken the next step without really intending to. Why did he kiss her like that? Chad shook his head. He'd gotten caught up in the excitement of the moment, that's all. He glared at Boy Wonder, as if it was the horse's fault for winning his race.

Well, it didn't matter, Chad told himself. They'd both agreed to forget it ever happened. But he wasn't sure he really wanted to forget. The memory caused a tightening in the groin. He frowned and began pacing the stall.

Jenny returned. "You sure look gloomy, Chad. Did Boy get injured during the race?"

"Boy's as fit as a fiddle. And I couldn't be more pleased." He stretched his lips into a smile to prove it.

"That was some race he ran, huh? If Boy gets to set the pace right out of the gate no one can come near him."

"Boy's a champ, no doubt about it," Jenny said. "Budenberry had the easiest ride of his career when he brought him home today." Her voice became peevish. "How come you give Willie the easy mounts and me the refusers, Chad?"

"It just worked out that way today. You know I don't play favorites with either the horses or the jocks, Jenny."

"That's not what everybody else thinks. You've heard the rumors going around about us, haven't you?"

Chad shrugged. "What do rumors matter so long as they're not true. Don't let them get to you, Jenny."

"But that's what gets to me the most, Chad. That they're *not* true!"

"Come off it, Jenny. You got over your schoolgirl crush on me years ago."

Jenny sighed dramatically. "Was that all it was, Chad? At the time I thought it was true love. How come you never took advantage of the situation?"

"Because it *would* have been taking advantage. You were just a kid back then."

"You weren't much older."

"But a lot more experienced."

"Weren't you ever just a teeny bit tempted?" She gave him an exaggerated wink.

Chad smiled at her goading. "I'd be a liar if I said I wasn't. You're as pretty as they come, Jenny. But one of the first rules I made for myself when I started here was never to mix business with pleasure. And being a man of steel, I stuck to it."

She laughed. "Men of steel have been known to melt when the right woman comes along."

"Is that right? Come to think of it, I've noticed Doc Revera looking a little melted around the edges lately. You got anything to do with that, Jenny?"

She fiddled with her hair. "Juan Revera is a fine veterinarian," she replied blandly although her cheeks had turned pink. "I have a great respect for his profession."

"Cut the double talk, Jenny. You're wild about the guy. I've seen the way you look at him, and looks don't lie."

She immediately turned the tables on him. "I've noticed *you* looking at somebody that way lately. You can't keep your eyes off her, and I'll bet you can't keep your hands off, either."

"You're way off track, Jenny."

"Am I? Then how come you don't even have to ask me who I'm talking about?"

Chad didn't bother answering that.

"She's nice enough, I suppose," Jenny allowed. "But Emily Holt is an outsider, Chad. She'll never feel comfortable in our world or understand what makes you tick."

"No one's asking her to," Chad replied gruffly. And the subject was closed as far as he was concerned.

Emily hurried into the Italian restaurant to find Roger waiting in the foyer. He made a big show of looking at his watch when she arrived.

"I'm terribly sorry I'm late," she said. "But I got tied up in traffic, and it couldn't be helped."

"It couldn't be?" He looked skeptical. "Where were you coming from?"

Emily hesitated. "Pacific Downs."

"The racetrack?" Roger's pale blue eyes grew wide.

"You needn't look so astonished," Emily said. "Horse racing is perfectly legal."

"Well, of course. But you don't seem the type to go in for that sort of thing, Emily."

She immediately became defensive. "What sort of thing?"

"Betting on horses."

"Oh, I didn't bet on any."

"Then why did you go? You must have better things to do than watch horses run around a track all day." Roger's tone implied that he certainly did.

Emily hadn't told him about inheriting a share in a racehorse because she hadn't planned on holding on to it. Now that she'd changed her mind she still felt disinclined to tell anyone. But Roger's superior attitude got the better of her natural reserve.

"Actually, I'm part owner of a horse that was entered in a race today." It gave her a thrill to be able to say that.

"Really?" Roger looked duly impressed. "Well, that's a horse of a different color." Laughing at his own wit, he motioned to the maître d' and they were led to their table.

As they walked to it Roger whisked his hand back and forth across Emily's back. She glanced over her shoulder with a questioning look.

"Appears to be a smudge of mud," he whispered.

"A what?" And then Emily remembered Chad giving her a consoling pat on the back.

"Don't worry. I brushed it off," Roger said.

Perhaps the visible evidence, Emily thought. But she feared that Chad had left a deeper mark on her that couldn't be brushed off so easily.

And sure enough, all through dinner, Emily found herself comparing Roger and every other man in the dining room to Chad Barron. They were all found sadly wanting. It was unfair, she knew, to dwell on the memory of one man as another wined and dined her. Unfair but uncontrollable. The harder she tried not to think about Chad, the more she did.

Forcing herself to focus her attention on Roger, she realized that he was waiting for her to respond to something he'd said. But that would be difficult. She hadn't heard a word.

"I'm sorry, Roger. Could you repeat that?"

He smiled indulgently. "You're a million miles away tonight, aren't you, Emily?"

More like ten, she thought. That was about the distance from the restaurant to the backstretch. "My mind sort of drifted," she admitted.

"I understand. You're thinking about him, aren't you?"

"Him?"

"Should I have said her? That racehorse of yours."

"No, Thunderbolt is a colt. He's called that because he has a blaze shaped like a streak of lightning." Emily leaned forward, more animated than she'd been all evening. Roger had touched on one of the two subjects for which she had recently developed a fascination. "He's a fine looking animal," she continued. "The moment I saw him I knew he was something special. He's independent to a fault, though. Won't let anybody tell him what to do. That makes him difficult to handle. But I believe he'll come around. I can see it in his eyes. When we looked at each other today there was a silent communication. An understanding. No words were needed. They would have gotten in the way."

Roger chuckled. "You sound as if you're talking about a *person* rather than a horse, Emily."

That stopped her dead. Roger was right. She could have just as well been talking about Chad. "I didn't mean to rattle on," she said.

"That's all right. Your enthusiasm is charming." Roger covered her hand with his. "I find you extremely charming, Emily dear. Don't you think we've reached the stage in our relationship where we should become more than friends?"

He was really a very nice man, she thought. A trifle stuffy perhaps. And overly concerned about the trappings of success. But he was attractive and attentive—the perfect companion really. Except his touch left her cold.

She slid her hand away from his and smiled wanly. "I think we should continue to stay friends, Roger. I don't see our relationship progressing beyond that."

"Perceptions can change," he replied.

Emily didn't argue. Perhaps he was right. Given enough time, perhaps she could develop warmer feelings for Roger.

They dropped the subject and finished their espresso. When they made their way out of the restaurant Roger halted Emily in the dimly lit foyer and swayed toward her. She allowed him to kiss her on the lips. His breath smelled of coffee and after-dinner mints. The kiss was not unpleasant but left Emily unmoved.

She stepped away from him. "Thank you for a lovely evening."

"It doesn't have to end," Roger said.

He walked Emily to her car and offered to follow her home. She told him it wasn't necessary, and he didn't persist. Emily liked him even better for that but knew for certain that she could never love him. If Roger had stood any chance at all to win her heart he had lost it when she compared his kiss to the one she'd shared with Chad Barron. What rotten luck, she thought ruefully, that the man whose touch pleased her to the core was absolutely the wrong one for her.

When Emily returned to her apartment she found Sachet, as usual, curled up on her bed. When she extended her hand to pet the cat, he sprang away and scuttled under the bed.

His odd behavior perplexed Emily. She lay stomach-down on the carpet and stuck her head under the bed. Sachet glared at her with accusing feline eyes.

"Come out, it's all right," she coaxed. But he wouldn't budge. The phone rang and Emily bumped her head on the bed frame as she got up to answer it. Because of this her tone was impatient when she said hello.

"Sounds like I caught you at a bad time, Emmie."

Her heart did a flip-flop. "Not at all, Chad," she said with the utmost casualness. She wasn't going to pretend she didn't know who it was.

"Are you alone?"

"Yes. Why do you ask?"

"I wouldn't want to interrupt anything."

"You aren't. I was just trying to get my cat out from under the bed. I can't understand it. He won't let me touch him." Oh, stop babbling like an idiot about your dumb cat, Emily chastised herself.

But Chad seemed interested. "Is that so? I reckon it's because he smells horses on you, and he's either jealous or scared."

"Well, what can I do about it?"

"Take all your clothes off."

"I beg your pardon?"

"Take all your clothes off, honey," Chad repeated in a languorous, exaggerated drawl. "And then go take a nice hot bath. After you get out rub some sweet-smelling lotion all over that lovely body of yours. That should make your cat happier."

Emily was almost purring herself. She didn't let on, though. "Thanks for the suggestion. I hope it works. I don't know if I could fall asleep without Sachet curled up at my feet."

"He sleeps in bed with you?" Chad laughed softly, filling her ear with the deep sound of his amusement. "That's one doggone lucky cat, Emmie."

She had no reply to that.

Chad's voice became more businesslike. "The reason I called is to tell you that I'm entering Thunder in a race this coming Friday."

"That soon? Are you sure he's ready to run again?"

"Racehorses are born ready. The whole purpose of their existence is to run."

"But I thought you were going to work with him before he competed again."

"I will," Chad assured her. "But Thunder shouldn't get time off for bad behavior, you know."

"No, but he needs time to overcome his anxiety at the starting gate, doesn't he?"

"Practice makes perfect, Emmie. You can't go easy on a horse because he starts acting up."

"Well, I hope you're not going to be tough on him because of it, either."

Chad groaned. "I'm a trainer, not a nursemaid. If Thunder's going to pay his way for us, he's got to run and win purses. It's as simple as that."

"But—"

"No buts about it, Emmie. I called to keep you informed, not to argue with you."

"I guess I was under the false impression that this was a discussion, not an argument."

"No, you were under the false impression that there's *room* for discussion."

Chad's domineering tone made Emily clutch the receiver tighter. "Don't I have any say whatsoever in this partnership?"

"No." His reply resounded in her ear. "I explained right off to you that this was a limited partnership, Emmie. I let people invest in my horses on the condition that I call all the shots."

"Well, I don't like that condition and I never agreed to it."

"But your father did."

That silenced Emily for a moment.

"You leave the handling of Thunder to me and everything will work out just fine," Chad advised. "All you have to do is come to see him race Friday. You can sit in my box."

"I have to work Friday. I can't go trotting off to the racetrack any time I please." Emily could hear how querulous she sounded now but she didn't care. Why should she be pleasant to a tyrant?

"And I can't arrange Thunder's racing schedule around your work schedule," Chad retorted. "Did you enjoy your dinner date tonight?"

His non sequitur threw her off and she answered honestly, without thinking. "Not particularly."

"Good." With that, Chad hung up on her.

Emily slammed down her own receiver, wishing she had beat him to the punch. He was overbearing, bull headed and rude to boot. If she never saw him again, it would be too soon. It seemed a shame that she would miss Thunderbolt's race, though. But the responsibilities of her job came first. Didn't they? Of course they did. And if there was one thing she prided herself on, it was being responsible.

"Emily! I'm glad you could make it today." Flo, seated in the first row of Chad's box, waved gaily. She was wearing a purple straw hat trimmed with orange peonies. An elderly man in a somber black suit was seated beside her.

Emily wondered if the man was another of her father's racetrack pals. She hoped so. Ever since she had heard what Flo and Sam Seager had to say about her father, she'd been more at peace with her memories of him. To know that Edmund Holt had not stopped caring about her meant a lot to Emily.

"Yes, I made it after all," she told Flo, greeting her with a light kiss on the cheek. Although she hadn't known Flo long she felt a connection with her, almost as if she were family.

Flo beamed at her. "So you're playing hooky from work, you naughty girl."

In fact, Emily had taken an official vacation day, but Flo seemed so delighted with her truancy that

Emily didn't want to disillusion her. "I couldn't possibly miss Thunderbolt's race today," she said.

The man in the black suit sniffed. "If indeed he *does* race. I hope I haven't come all the way out here to witness another fiasco."

Emily's hackles immediately rose. What right had this stranger to cast aspersions on her fine horse?

"Emily, I'd like you to meet Dr. Peterson," Flo said. "Be careful what you say to him because he's a shrink." Peterson winced at that description, but Flo didn't seem to notice. "Doctor, this is Emily Holt. One of our partners."

"Oh, yes." He gave Emily a curt nod. "I believe you called me a while back about selling your share of the horse, Ms. Holt."

"That's right." Emily recalled that the psychiatrist had pronounced Thunderbolt neurotic and himself insane for investing in such a recalcitrant horse. "But I've decided to hold on to my share," she told him.

He sniffed again. "I doubt anyone would buy it. The horse is obviously a loser."

Emily hoped Peterson had a more positive manner when dealing with patients. "Perhaps Thunderbolt hasn't proven himself yet," she said in a calm voice. "But I have high expectations."

"Hardly based on the reality of the situation, my dear," he commented dryly.

"The reality is that Thunderbolt has an excellent trainer," Emily shot back. Her ardent defense surprised her. She wasn't usually so combative. Who was she sticking up for? she wondered. Thunderbolt or Chad?

"Yes, I know all about Barron's fine reputation as a trainer," Dr. Peterson responded in a bored tone.

"That's why I invested in the horse in the first place. But I think Barron's let success go to his head and now he's spreading himself too thin. He may have a stable full of horses, but he only has time to devote to the winners. Losers like Thunderbolt fall by the wayside."

Emily couldn't refute that because she had little knowledge of how Chad operated. In fact, the doctor's cliché-ridden opinions touched on her own apprehensions. Hadn't she gotten the impression last Saturday that Chad favored his prize horse Boy Wonder over Thunderbolt? Of course that was only natural, considering he had bred Boy. Emily could understand that. Still, she didn't want *her* horse to be slighted.

"Thunder has never actually lost a race," she pointed out to the doctor.

"Hah! A mere technicality. That's only because he's refused to run in one."

"He has great workout times," Flo put in, waving her racing form.

"That doesn't count," Dr. Peterson retorted. "Workout times don't earn us a red cent, now do they?"

"But they prove Thunder has the ability," Flo countered.

"The proof is in the pudding," Dr. Peterson pronounced and began perusing his own racing form, lips pursed.

"Let's go down to the paddock and wish Thunder well," Emily said to Flo in a low voice, hoping to exclude the dour doctor.

"Oh, it's too early for that," Flo said. "Thunder is in the next to the last race and won't get saddled for another hour or so. He's still in the barn."

"Could we go see him there?"

Flo shook her head. "I don't think Chad would appreciate that. He barely tolerates us investors as it is, you know."

"Only too well," Emily muttered.

But Flo wasn't listening. "Dixie Cupcake's odds keep dropping," she commented, studying the infield tote board flashing the current odds for the next race. "I think I'll get in on the action. I don't suppose you want to come place a bet with me, sweetie?"

"No thanks. You go ahead, Flo."

Being left alone with Dr. Peterson didn't ease her anxiety about Thunderbolt's upcoming race. The psychiatrist kept shaking his head and mumbling to himself as he read the racing form. He made a point of ignoring Emily, and she guessed that he resented her for disagreeing with him. She grew uncomfortable sitting beside his stony silence and decided to take a walk. She excused herself, but he didn't bother to look up when she left the box.

Emily strolled through the grandstand crowds, soaking up the atmosphere. Food and drink stands abounded, as did closed circuit TVs to view the races without ever going outside. People lined up at the betting windows. Emily looked for Flo's big purple hat but couldn't spot it in the crowd.

She could feel an undercurrent of excitement all around her. People's faces reflected it. It occurred to Emily that racing was really a participatory sport. The fans affected the odds and profited or lost from the outcome.

So this was her father's milieu, she mused. He must have thrived on the excitement—or at least preferred it to anything else in his life, including his family. She remembered her parents' constant bickering. Their marriage had not been a happy one. Emily had always assumed that her father's gambling problem had been the cause of their misery together, but maybe there had been more to it than that. She would never know the whole story. Edmund Holt had died without explaining himself to her. Perhaps he'd avoided contacting her because he had no explanations.

Emily pictured him milling through this crowd, buying a hot dog at the stand she passed, then ambling up to the betting windows and eating it as he waited in line to put down his last few bucks. She saw him as she remembered him from twenty years ago— a big handsome man with dark wavy hair and an easy smile. He'd never raised his voice to her, let alone his hand. He'd called her his good luck charm. He'd made her laugh. He'd made her feel safe. And she had loved him with all her heart. That hadn't stopped him from abandoning her, though. He had left her to go off and gamble his life away.

Calling up his image brought back all the pain of his abandonment, and Emily suddenly felt the loss as sharply as she had as a child. She stopped, mid-stride, as people swirled around her in every direction. She felt a fool to have this strong reaction now, as an adult. Would she ever get over it?

She inhaled deeply. Of course she was over it, she told herself. She would be all right as soon as she got out of this environment where the ghost of her father hovered like an all-encompassing fog.

Emily hurried outside, and the warm spring sun on her back comforted her. She continued walking at a brisk pace, not paying much attention to where she was headed. When she found herself on the tree-lined road leading to the barn area, she kept going until a guard stopped her at the gate.

"Do you have a pass?" he asked her.

"No, but I'm part owner of a horse stabled here. I'd like to see him before he races."

"Can't let you in without a pass."

It suddenly became important to Emily to be allowed inside. "Could you put in a call to Chad Barron? He'll vouch for me."

"Mr. Barron trains your horse?" The guard smiled for the first time.

"Yes. Tell him Emmie Holt would like to see Thunderbolt."

"Wait right here. I'll give him a call."

He went inside the gatehouse, and Emily could see him in the open doorway, dialing a phone. The conversation was short. When the guard returned, he wasn't smiling anymore. "Sorry, Ms. Holt. Permission denied."

"Oh." Emily felt the heat of humiliation sting her face but she made sure she kept her shoulders straight and her chin high as she walked away.

Chapter Seven

Chad, on his sturdy Appaloosa, ponied Thunderbolt to the starting gate. His handlers usually led the runners to post, but Chad was giving Thunderbolt special treatment today. He had spent most of the week working with the unpredictable colt. Instead of saddling Thunder with an exercise rider, Chad had ridden beside him every morning, leading him on a rope. He wanted to make Thunder feel secure enough to get through a race. Hoping to keep him calm today, Chad had equipped him with blinkers and put cotton in his ears to dull the noise of the crowd.

"You sure are babying this horse," Jenny commented from atop Thunderbolt. "You think he's worth it, Chad?"

"Time will tell," he replied, keeping a firm hold of Thunder's lead as his pony trotted alongside. "I do know that we stand a good chance of winning today, Jenny. You're aboard the best horse in the field.''

"You said that the last time I rode him, Chad. I think you've got a thing for this horse." Jenny slid her goggles down. "Or maybe you got a thing for one of his owners, hmm?"

"Stop riding me about Emmie Holt. Just concentrate on riding Thunder to the finish line first."

Chad's tone was light but his mood wasn't. Disappointment weighed him down. He'd expected Emmie to show up at the paddock before the race even though she had told him she had to work. Hell, couldn't she take off a few hours to see her horse run? Especially today, when Thunder stood such a good chance of winning.

The whole time Chad had been showering the animal with time and attention, he'd been thinking about Emmie—how it would please her to see her horse come in first. And she hadn't even bothered to show up for the race! That showed downright indifference as far as Chad was concerned. All Emmie's talk about being so concerned over Thunder's welfare was just that . . . talk.

Chad sidetracked this train of thought. What did he care if Emmie showed up today or not? Investors were a pain in the neck when they became involved with the horses. The last thing he wanted was for them to start hanging around the backstretch, getting in his way, interfering with the way he ran things. Still, he sure wouldn't have minded a visit from Emmie in the paddock.

Still fuming about Chad's refusal to grant her entry to his barn, Emily sat rigid in her box seat and watched him accompany Thunderbolt and Jenny to the starting gate.

"I see that Mr. Barron has taken to escorting a certain jockey around the track," she couldn't help observing aloud. "Since when do trainers act as pony boys?" Her tone was so caustic that Flo looked at her askance.

"Chad must have his reasons," she told Emily. "And maybe we would have found out what they were if we had gone to the paddock before the race. Why didn't you want to, sweetie?"

Emily hadn't told Flo about being turned away by the guard earlier. She was too hurt to talk about it. And too mortified. "I wasn't in the mood," she answered lamely. "But you could have gone with Dr. Peterson, Flo."

"Oh, pooh, visiting the paddock is old hat to me." Flo adjusted her new one, folding back the straw brim. "It's only fun when you come along, Emily. You seemed to get such a kick out of it last time."

"Yes, it was an interesting experience," Emily said. "But I don't like to go where I'm not wanted."

"You mean because of the way Moss acted last Saturday? Don't pay him any mind, Emily. He's just a cantankerous old fool."

Emily knew that and could easily ignore Moss's hostility. At least he was open about it. Chad, on the other hand, blew hot and cold. He could be so charming one moment, so distant the next. Emily wished that she could forget the incident with the guard. What did it matter if Chad had turned her away from his barn? Her heart tightened. It mattered a lot.

Flo nudged Emily's arm with her elbow. "Speaking of cantankerous old fools," she whispered. "Here comes another one."

Dr. Peterson returned to the box and sat beside Flo. "While I was in the paddock I had a long chat with Barron's foreman Moss," he said. "Now there's a man who knows what he's talking about."

"Takes one to know one," Flo said, nudging Emily again.

Assuming he'd been complimented, Peterson nodded. "Moss is sure Thunderbolt would perform better under the guidance of a stronger, more experienced jockey."

"Moss just doesn't like women," Flo said.

"If Jessup were a *man,* though," Peterson countered, "would Barron be so inclined to give her another chance with our horse, I wonder."

Emily also wondered about that, but she bit the inside of her lip and said nothing. Instead, she watched with bated breath as an assistant starter took Thunderbolt's lead from Chad and walked the horse the rest of the way to post. Thunder went into his slot like a lamb, and the back gate closed behind him. At least he was in, she thought with relief. Now all he had to do was go out. A moment later the buzzer shrieked, the front gates flapped open and the horses boomed onto the track. Thunderbolt broke well and immediately took the lead.

"He's running!" Emily cried, jumping up from her seat. "He's actually running!"

But her joy was short-lived. Thunderbolt suddenly swerved to the right, made a U-turn, and began running in the wrong direction. Terrified, Emily dug her teeth into her clenched fist and prayed that he wouldn't ram into an oncoming horse. Luckily, he steered clear of the rest of the field, then slowed down to a casual trot once they had passed. The spectators began hooting. An outrider galloped onto the track, caught up with Thunder, and helped Jenny guide him off the raceway and into the gap. Emily recognized the outrider's broad back and dappled pony. Chad.

"Good Lord! What happened to him this time?" Flo said.

"I thought I saw him foaming at the mouth," Dr. Peterson said.

"I didn't see that," Emily said, but her apprehension grew.

"I've heard of racehorses going completely crazy," Peterson continued in his bored voice. "When they become uncontrollable like that they start kicking at anything in sight. The only way to stop them is to shoot them."

"Shoot them!" Emily cried.

"With a sedative, my dear. Before they do harm to themselves or others."

"I don't think Thunderbolt went bonkers," Flo said in her reasonable voice.

"Well, what would you call running the wrong way down a track?" Peterson countered. "He could have been so spooked that he injured himself."

Emily had heard enough of his dismal conjecture. "I'm going to find out what happened to Thunder right now!"

She left the box and ran all the way from the clubhouse to the backstretch gate.

"You again," the guard said.

"You must let me go to Barron's barn," Emily told him. "I have to find out what happened to my horse during his race."

"Please stay calm, miss," he advised. "I'll put in another call to Mr. Barron's office."

Emily had no intention of being turned away by Chad again. When the guard went into the gatehouse she hiked up her short straight skirt, climbed over the fence, and ran up the path toward the barns. As soon as he realized what had happened, the guard began chasing after her, but he was overweight and out of shape and no match for an ex-sprinter. Thankful she'd worn flat shoes, Emily left him in the dust.

Chad had a deep frown on his face as he came around his barn. It changed to a widening grin when he saw Emily Holt running down the path like a bat out of hell. No—more like a vision out of heaven, he decided. She was still a good distance away but he reckoned he could spot Emmie from a mile. Her long russet hair was like a flag gleaming in the sunshine. And those long legs. Nobody but Emmie had legs as fine as that.

Boy, she really could run, Chad observed with the utmost approval. Resting the saddle he was carrying against his hip, he watched her intently. She had all the makings of a champion, he decided—perfect form, fine spirit, and that ineffable quality, *class*.

Enchanted by the sight of her, it took Chad a while to notice that a man seemed to be chasing her from about ten lengths behind and losing ground steadily. Hey, wasn't that George the gate guard? Whoever he was, the man gave up the chase and limped away in the opposite direction. Chad turned his eyes back to Emmie. She was coming up fast, heading for the homestretch. He waved to get her attention and put down his saddle, ready to reward her efforts with a big hug.

Emily stopped a few feet short of him. And the way she glared at Chad didn't make him inclined to put his arms around her. Unable to speak for a moment, she gulped air, chest heaving.

"I didn't expect to see you today," Chad said in a casual tone, as if a woman running madly toward him and then gasping for breath was nothing unusual. He smiled as he watched her pert breasts rise and fall beneath her soft ribbed sweater.

"Where's Thunderbolt?" she demanded as soon as she could speak.

Chad cocked a thumb in a belt loop of his jeans. "Being cooled out. Why don't we drop the Thunder and change his name to plain Bolt?"

Emily continued to glare at him. "Very funny. Is he all right?"

"He's fine, honey."

"Are you sure? He looked so terrified running the wrong way."

"So was everyone else, believe me. But we managed to settle him down just fine."

"Can I see him?"

"Sure. Bobby should be washing him now. He got up quite a lather during his brief run. Considering how well he broke, it's a damn shame he went wild on us." Chad took in Emily's tousled hair and flushed face. "You look kinda wild yourself, Emmie." His eyes roamed to her short skirt and legs. "You know, I was real disappointed when you didn't show up at the paddock before Thunder's race today."

So he was trying out his charm routine with her again, Emily thought, her gold eyes hardening. First he refuses to let her enter the back side, and when she manages to break in anyway, he acts as if he's pleased to see her. What a phony.

"Cut the bull," she told him.

Chad raised his dark eyebrows. "Why, Emmie. How unlike you."

"Listen, we need to get a few things straight."

His eyebrows shot up another notch. "Name one."

"Your high-handed manner when dealing with your partners. We have our rights."

"Name one," he said again.

"We should have an input in decisions concerning Thunderbolt."

"Decisions? Name one."

"Don't try to stonewall me, Barron."

"I'm just waiting for you to get to the point. Catch your breath and take all the time you need. I'm a patient man."

His patronizing attitude infuriated Emily. Her heart pumped hard—from the run, from anger, from his very presence. Blood rushing to her head drove out caution.

"All right, you asked for it, mister. I'll get to the point," she said. "Stop letting your personal relationships interfere with your job as a trainer."

Chad narrowed his eyes. "Meaning what?"

"Jenny Jessup. She obviously can't handle Thunderbolt. I've witnessed her failure two times in a row and I don't want my horse put at risk again."

Chad shook his head as if truly disappointed. "You're as prejudiced as the *men* around here."

"That's not true!" Emily protested. "I simply think Thunder would stand a better chance at winning with a different jockey. I don't care if you choose another female as long as she's not one of your girlfriends!''

"You're overstepping, Emmie," Chad warned. He widened his stance and crossed his arms over his chest.

Emily widened her own stance and placed her fists on her hips. "Overstepping what? My lowly position as a *limited* partner? Well, I'm sick and tired of your absolute monarchy, Barron. I'm going to organize a rebellion."

Without moving, without so much as blinking, they stared at each other as horses and backstretch workers passed by. Neither of them noticed. The rest of the world had ceased to exist as they locked horns.

Emily did her best to keep from showing any sign of weakness. Chad did his best to keep from smiling. A rebellion? What was she fixing to do? Organize a horse sit-in?

Much to Emily's surprise, Chad gave in first and looked away. Something had caught his attention behind her. His eyes began twinkling at the sight. Emily turned around, expecting to see Jenny coming up the road. Instead she saw the gate guard driving up in a truck. He braked to a screeching stop and got out, expression grim.

"I'm real sorry about this, Mr. Barron," he said, jutting his double chin in Emily's direction. "She climbed over the fence while I was calling your office."

"Did she now?" Chad maintained a straight face.

"I tried catching up to her but she was too fast for me."

"You gotta watch out for these fast women, George," Chad said in a commiserative tone.

"Claims she owns one of the horses in your barn," the guard reported.

Chad sighed. "All these racetrack groupies claim that."

A groupie? Emily seethed. "Stop talking nonsense, Chad," she demanded.

Chad ignored her and sidled up to the guard. "I just can't keep them away from me, George," he said in a hushed tone. "Some women have a *thing* for horse trainers."

"Yeah, that must be tough, Mr. Barron." George winked. "You want I should take her away?"

Chad made a great show of mulling this over as Emily glowered at him. "Naw, let her stay. She looks harmless enough," he finally told George. "Sorry she caused you all this trouble, though."

"It sure beats playing solitaire." George gave Emily an appreciative look, winked at Chad again and walked back to his truck.

"Wipe that disgusting grin off your face," Emily told Chad, truly wishing that looks could kill.

"Come on, honey, where's your sense of humor?"

"I don't find being the butt of your idiotic jokes the least bit amusing." Her voice quavered slightly.

Chad looked mildly contrite. "Well, I didn't go and let George haul you away, now did I. Why'd you go and jump that fence anyway?"

"Because that's the only way I could get in! I wasn't going to meekly stand by and have you tell George to turn me away again."

"What are you talking about, Emmie? I would never turn you away."

Emily couldn't believe his gall. "Stop lying to me," she implored. It hurt her even more than his refusal to let her in had. "At least be honest enough to own up to your own actions."

Anger suddenly sparked in Chad's eyes. "Dammit, Emmie, I'm not lying." He shouted to George as he was pulling away.

George got out of the truck and came back again. "Change your mind about her already, Mr. Barron?"

"We have to straighten something out with this lady right now," Chad told him. "Did you turn Ms. Holt away earlier today when she asked to visit my barn?"

"Sure did." The guard smirked. "She's a persistent one all right."

Chad frowned at him and his smirk vanished. "Since when do you have the authority to turn away people who want to see me, George?"

"Hey, I followed procedure!" he protested. "I called your office and checked her out. Moss told me to send her away because you were busy, so I did."

"Moss?"

The guard nodded. "Isn't he next in charge at your barn? According to my list he is."

"Okay, George, you did your job," Chad allowed. "I got no bone to pick with *you*."

The guard looked relieved.

"But this lady should be let through to my barn any time she pleases." Chad put his arm around Emily's shoulder. "I was just kidding around before. Ms. Holt really does own a share of one of the horses I train. I'll get her an official pass first thing Monday morning."

"Hey, she won't even have to show it to me, Mr. Barron. I'll remember her for sure." George smiled sheepishly at Emily. "From now on any time you feel like climbing over the fence is fine with me, Ms. Holt."

"I won't make a habit of it," Emily assured him.

"I'm real sorry this happened," Chad told Emily after George drove off again.

She believed him and leaned into his solid body, enjoying the secure weight of his arm around her shoulders. Her heart sang with the knowledge that Chad hadn't refused her entry to his backstretch world after all. Realizing how much it meant to her, Emily grew uneasy. She couldn't allow herself to care that much about how this man regarded her. She forced herself to draw away from him.

"I'm glad we cleared everything up," she said coolly. "At least now George knows that I'm not some crazy woman chasing after you."

"Hey, I'm sorry about that, too. Sometimes I get a little carried away with my teasing." Chad smiled disarmingly. "You really think a woman has to be crazy to go chasing after me?"

Emily didn't smile back. "Absolutely. You're an intolerant despot."

Chad shrugged off the description. "Not always. Only when it comes to my barn." He moved to put his arm around her again. "What do you say to calling a truce, Emmie?"

Emily stepped back. "No way, Chad. I still intend to fight you about the way you're handling Thunderbolt."

His disarming smile became a dangerous one. "Mind telling me how you aim to do that?"

"Not at all. I'm planning to call a meeting of all the shareholders. Since you happen to be one of them, you'll be included, of course."

"That's downright democratic of you."

"That's the whole idea. Now may I please see my horse?"

Without replying, Chad picked up his saddle, balanced it against his hip, and began walking away from her.

Emily studied the stubborn set of his broad shoulders, the rigid posture of his back, and sighed. Impossible man. At the same time she thought this, she couldn't help but appreciate how his low-riding jeans molded to his narrow hips and tight round butt. Like the Thoroughbreds he trained, Chad Barron had a splendid physique.

Without breaking the rhythm of his long, easy stride he looked over his shoulder. "You going to stand there all day, Emmie? Or are you going to come along with me?"

Emily had to trot to catch up with him. "You enjoy keeping me off balance, don't you, Chad?"

"Is that what I do to you? I don't mean to." He quickly glanced at her, then looked straight ahead again. "You're the one trying to throw things off balance around here, honey. I'm more than a little put out about this meeting idea of yours."

"Well, you shouldn't be. It's nothing personal."

"Yes, it is," he insisted. His obstinate expression seemed set in stone.

Chad continued walking without saying another word. He'd decided to drop the subject for the time being, hoping this notion of hers would blow over. He wasn't accustomed to arguing with women, mainly because they'd mostly seen eye to eye with him. Until Emmie. She was different. He brought her to a grassy area behind his barn where Thunderbolt was being bathed by Bobby Lee.

"Well, lookie who's here," Bobby said.

As if understanding, Thunderbolt actually did turn his head to look in Emily's direction. Then he whinnied and did a little two-step dance.

She clapped her hands, delighted. "I'm happy to see you, too, Thunder. Are you okay?"

"He's fine now, Miss Holt," Bobby said. "Just got a little mixed up is all."

"You want to try your hand at bathing him?" Chad asked her.

Emily looked skeptical. "Do you think I could manage it, Chad?"

He smiled. "Honey, you don't have to be a rocket scientist to wash down a horse. Heck, even a dolt like Bobby Lee can manage it."

"Thanks a bunch." Bobby threw his wet sponge at his uncle. "Why don't you take over, Einstein?"

"Be happy to. And while Emmie and I see to Thunder, why don't you go supervise the 'scrub the feed tubs' department?"

"Meaning why don't I go and scrub them myself," Bobby muttered.

"Get some of the grooms lying about to help you," Chad suggested. "If you finish early, you can quit for the day."

"All *right!*" Bobby agreed and hurried off.

"Bobby's learning this business from the bottom up," Chad told Emily. "I'm hoping to make him my foreman some day."

"What about Moss?"

"I'm also hoping he'll want to retire in a few years. I plan to set him up with a nice pension when he does.

But I'm not going to turn him out to pasture before he's good and ready, even though we don't see eye to eye all the time." Chad caught himself. What was he doing, confiding in Emily Holt like this? He rarely confided in anyone, let alone a mutinous limited partner. "Anyway, Moss was out of line when he told George to turn you away. I'll be sure to tell him so, Emmie."

"Forget it," she said. "It's over and done with and I don't want to be the cause of friction between you and your foreman."

So she wasn't vindictive, Chad thought. Good for her. Thunderbolt snorted. "You getting impatient, sport? Okay, we'll finish you up. Emmie, you wash his near side."

"Which is?"

"His left side," Chad replied, shaking his head over her ignorance as he rolled up the sleeves of his work shirt. "You don't know the first thing about these animals. Yet you presume to know more about how to handle them than I do. First time I laid eyes on you I figured you for a troublemaker, you know."

"Really?" Emily stopped staring at his sinewy, tanned forearms and lifted her eyes to his face. "Why on earth did you assume that?"

Because when he'd spotted her by the rail as he'd passed aboard Thunder, he'd felt a sharp tightening in his heart. But Chad didn't tell her that. He didn't answer her at all. Instead, he dunked the sponge in the red rubber bucket and squeezed it out.

Emily couldn't help wonder if Chad was imagining that he was twisting her neck instead of the sponge. "Chad, I just want to have a meeting about Thunder. Is that so terrible?"

"Depends on what comes of it." He passed the sponge over Thunder, from withers to loin, and the wet coat shone like black satin. "See, that's all there is to it." He tossed Emily the sponge.

Following his example, she swirled the sponge in the water, which smelled of mint and antiseptic. She wrung it out and slid it across Thunderbolt, feeling the solid form of the beast under her hand. It thrilled her almost as much as the sight of Chad's muscular, dark-haired forearms had.

Chad silently watched Emily wash the horse, amused at how careful she was to cover each inch of him with the soapy water. Her nice linen sweater and skirt were getting splattered but she didn't seem to mind. She hadn't minded getting her hands muddied up, either, he recalled. Maybe she was a lot more earthy than he'd originally surmised. One thing for sure—she had spunk. Jumping over that fence in defiance of the guard definitely took spunk.

Emily glanced over her shoulder. "What are you grinning about?"

"Can't a man smile on such a beautiful spring day? Keep washing. You're doing a fine job."

"And what are *you* doing besides enjoying the day?"

"Supervising, honey. Don't forget to give Thunder's rump a nice rubdown."

"I thought we were going to do this together, Chad."

He spread open his hands in a helpless gesture. "Hey, there's only one sponge."

Emily rolled her eyes, then returned to washing the horse. "I don't really mind doing it by myself," she said.

In fact she loved it, Chad thought. Her every lithe movement demonstrated how much she was enjoying the experience of intimately connecting with the race-horse. Her russet hair looked even brighter against Thunder's slick black coat, he noted. And her body looked even more fine boned and delicate alongside such a muscular steed. Chad felt a stirring in his groin. Until this moment, he had never considered the simple task of washing a horse such a sensual act. But watching Emily Holt do it made him almost envious of Thunderbolt.

"That's good enough," he said gruffly, taking the sponge from her. He did the horse's off side with brisk efficiency. "Now we scrape him."

Chad picked up an aluminum scraper and showed Emily how to whisk off the excess soap from Thunderbolt's body. She finished the task with as much diligence as she had washed the animal. Satisfied that not a particle of soap remained on the glossy coat, Emily stepped aside to admire Thunderbolt. Chad covered him with a faded plaid blanket.

"Don't want him to get cooled out too fast," he explained. "Now we walk him."

"Where?"

"Around and around the shed row for about forty-five minutes. Some trainers hook their horses up to hot-walking machines but I'm not partial to them. Too cold and mechanical. Horses deserve to be treated with tender care and consideration. Like us humans, they thrive on it."

Emily smiled softly. "Why, Chad, you really are sentimental when it comes to your horses."

That made him frown. "Not me. No way. I'm being smart, not sentimental. I don't want my Thoroughbreds getting injured on one of those infernal machines. Hell, I heard of horses hanging themselves on them. I'd rather pay someone to walk my stock rather than risk damaging such valuable property. No profit in *that!*"

Emily liked his first explanation better and preferred to believe that Chad was motivated by "care and consideration" more than profit. She continued to smile at him, as if they shared some kind of secret.

He bowed and offered his arm. "Care to go for a stroll, pretty lady?"

"Delighted," she said.

They promenaded along the wide aisle encompassing the outer edge of the stalls, Chad leading Thunderbolt by his shank. Horses stuck their heads over the Dutch doors to watch them pass as they munched hay. Like idle busybodies, Emily thought. Thunderbolt ignored them all with regal disdain until they neared a particular stall. Then he perked up considerably, tail lifting, ears pricked, and began vigorously nodding his head.

"He's got a thing for Rosie," Chad said to Emily. Sure enough, when a lovely chestnut filly poked her head out of the stall, Thunder began nickering in a low, pulsing tone.

"How sweet," Emily said as Thunder danced in front of Rosie's stall.

"I don't know how sweet it is," Chad grumbled. "I think the reason Thunder ran the wrong way in that race today was because he spotted Rosie being led to the paddock area just before he left it, and he wanted to go back to be with her."

"*Love* made him do it!" Emily clasped her hands and brought them to her chest. She gazed at the black colt with fond forgiveness. "Oh, Thunder, you crazy romantic."

"Crazy all right." Chad looked at the colt with disgust rather than forgiveness. "You can't let some filly interfere with your job, sport. And your job is to win races, dammit." He tugged at Thunder's shank and led him past pretty Rosie. The colt cast her a parting look of longing.

"Maybe you should have Rosie waiting at the finish line the next time Thunder races," Emily said.

"Listen, I'll be willing to give it a try if it were allowed. Anything to get this horse back on track!" Chad exhaled his exasperation. "Of course, my theory about Rosie is only conjecture. Could be that Thunder is just plain fractious."

Could be that he needs a more experienced jockey to guide him, Emily thought. She knew she'd get nowhere bringing this up with Chad again, though. She would need the backing of the three other investors to get this headstrong, freewheeling trainer to listen to reason.

Besides, she didn't want to argue with Chad anymore today. He had offered her a truce and she accepted it willingly now, at least on a temporary basis. Afternoon was a relatively peaceful time in the barn, compared to the hectic morning, and Emily was enjoying her shed row stroll with Chad and Thunder. Music, as always, played in the background, competing with the sounds of snorting, shuffling horses. Emily found herself almost gliding to the lilting tempo of it.

"I can't believe it!" she said. "You're playing waltzes for the horses!"

"I like to calm them down before their dinner," Chad told her in a practical tone. "They seem to enjoy Strauss."

"Do they? And how do they feel about Mozart?" she asked, trying not to smile because he seemed so serious.

"They prefer Chopin," he replied, straight-faced. "But I think what they really like hearing is female vocalists. Especially late at night. Linda Ronstadt, for instance."

So that's who Chad liked to listen to late at night, Emily surmised. She felt a warm pleasure in knowing this intimate detail about him. As she accidently brushed against him as they walked, this pleasure radiated from the pit of her stomach to the tips of her fingers and toes. Emily felt abashed that such a casual, unintended contact with him could shoot through her system like that.

"You'd better not let your heart overrule your head," Chad said softly.

Chapter Eight

Emily stared at Chad, wide-eyed and speechless. Had he actually been reading her mind?

"Your growing attachment is so obvious, Emmie," he continued. "Anybody with an ounce of brains in his head could spot it."

Emily flushed and looked away from him. She had thought she'd been doing such a good job of hiding how physically compelling she found him. How could he have guessed?

"Don't look so embarrassed about it," he said sympathetically. "It happens all the time. Women can't seem to help themselves."

Oh, the supreme egotism of this man! His blatant self-flattery diminished his appeal considerably. "I assure you *I* can help myself," she replied in a brittle voice.

Chad looked at her skeptically. "Easier said than done, honey. Now that you're smitten, you're going to want to start hanging around here all the time."

"Don't worry, Chad. I've got much better things to do, believe me!"

He sighed. "Once you get bitten by the bug, it's hard to shake. And females are so darn susceptible. I reckon they're pushovers for surpassing power and beauty."

"Surpassing power and beauty?" Emily repeated in a disbelieving voice. Ruggedly handsome he might be, but Chad was really getting carried away with himself now. "You've got to be kidding," she told him.

"I'm dead serious. In my humble opinion—"

Humble! She let out a hoot.

Frowning slightly at her interruption, Chad went on. "Racehorses are the most beautiful creatures on the face of the earth. And I know you feel that way about Thunderbolt, Emmie. I saw the way you were looking at him after his bath."

Thunderbolt? Emily quickly replayed their conversation in her mind. Realizing that Chad had been talking about the colt and not himself, she covered her face with her hands and groaned.

"Hey, don't be too hard on yourself." Chad hugged her briefly to comfort her. "It's perfectly normal to become attached to a racehorse. But you've got to always remember that Thunder is a business investment, Emmie."

Emily regained her composure, glad that Chad hadn't noticed how she'd misinterpreted him before. "I understand," she said. "And my heart isn't ruling my head. I think my request for a shareholders' meeting to discuss his future is perfectly reasonable."

"It's not the way we do things around here," Chad grumbled.

"*We* meaning *you,* of course."

"Okay. You win. I'll call a meeting next week."

"What?" Emily stopped walking, stunned.

Chad also stopped. "You heard me, honey. We can meet in my office." He smiled tightly. "Unless you consider it enemy territory."

"Your office will be fine, Chad. I don't consider you the enemy." She looked up at him with sincere regard. "I'm hoping we can all work together for Thunderbolt's good."

Chad slowly raised his hand and trailed a finger down Emily's cheek. "You're so naive," he said.

She barely heard him, her sense of touch overpowering all others. The rough grain of his fingertip sent a shiver up her spine.

Thunderbolt reared, apparently impatient with being ignored. Chad dropped his left hand from Emily's face and tightened his hold on the shank with his right. "Easy, sport. You've caused enough trouble for one day."

They continued to walk the shed row for a while longer, stopping now and then to let Thunderbolt take a drink of water. Chad remained silent and Emily wondered if he was brooding over his capitulation to her demand. She studied him from the corner of her eye but could tell nothing from his blank expression. Her cheek still tingled from his touch.

"Do you have a specific date in mind for this meeting?" she asked him, not wanting to press but needing to have his promise made more concrete.

"Soon," he said vaguely.

That wasn't good enough. "How soon? Before Thunder's next race, I hope."

"Soon!" he said again, impatiently this time. "Trust me on this, Emmie. I'll keep in touch."

They left it at that.

Chad sifted through invoices in his office that evening. He usually spent Saturday nights trying to catch up on bookkeeping. He found this part of his job tedious, but didn't trust anyone else to do it properly.

Linda Ronstadt's dulcet voice emanated from the speakers. She was singing old-time love ballads. Finding it difficult to concentrate, Chad leaned back in his chair and closed his eyes for a minute. He'd listened to this particular album many times before, but now every song on it conjured up golden images of Emily Holt—Emmie running...Emmie smiling... brushing back her curls...dunking her hands in a bucket of mud...washing Thunder.

Chad found her uninvited invasion into his thoughts irksome but irrepressible. He'd been dwelling on her way too much lately. Each time he saw her, he found something new to delight in and recall in quiet moments like this. When the phone rang and disrupted his reverie, he stared at it a long moment, slightly dazed. He answered on the fifth ring.

"Still working, honey?" a female voice inquired. "Don't you ever let up? Are you eating right? Are you getting enough sleep?"

Chad smiled wearily. "Hi, Ma. I'm fine."

"You don't sound fine. You sound bushed. You're driving yourself too hard. You're as bad as your father."

"No one could be as bad as him."

"You're birds of a feather but you're both too mule headed to admit it."

"Make up your mind, Ma," Chad teased. "Are we birds or mules?"

"You're Barrons, that's what. The stubbornest creatures in God's universe. Are you going to get him a present for his birthday?"

"Why should I? He can afford to buy anything he wants."

"But you sent me a lovely gift for mine."

"That's different, Ma. You and I are on speaking terms."

"Aw, honey, this breach with your father has got to end. Come home and mend your fences, son."

The wistfulness in his mother's voice seeped into Chad's heart and he had to swallow before answering. "I can't do that, Ma. He swore he'd have me kicked off the property if I ever set foot on it again."

"He didn't mean for you to stay away forever! But he's too proud to contact you. You're the one who'll have to put an end to this estrangement. It's gone on for long enough."

"Forget it, Ma." Chad hated being hard with her but he knew what she was fixing to spring on him and wanted to nip it in the bud. "I'm not coming back like some repentant prodigal son."

"Who said anything about being repentant or prodigal, Chadwick? I called to ask you—no, entreat you—to come to your father's birthday party next month."

"I figured as much. You gave your hand away when you suggested I get him a present."

"Please come, son. It's time to make peace with him. He won't live forever."

"Sure he will." But then Chad felt a stab of apprehension. "He's okay, isn't he? Not sick or anything?"

"Healthy as a horse. But no spring chicken."

Chad chuckled. "Is he still sly as a fox and strong as an ox?"

"Don't try to distract me by poking fun, Chadwick. Tell me that you'll come to his party. Half the county's invited."

"Then Pa doesn't need me there." Chad made an attempt to change the subject. "Bobby Lee has been doing a fine job for me here."

It worked. His mother couldn't resist asking all about her eldest grandchild. But after being assured of Bobby's emotional and physical well-being, she zeroed in on Chad's personal life.

"You shouldn't be working on a Saturday night, son. You should be out enjoying yourself in the company of some nice young lady."

Nice young lady, Chad knew, was his mother's euphemism for future daughter-in-law. "I don't have time for much of a personal life," he said.

"Then make time," she suggested in a sharper voice than normal. "Don't wait until middle age to settle down and start a family."

"Why not? Pa did."

"See, you're just like him. Two birds of a feather," she said again.

"No, we're not," Chad insisted. "I'd never disown a child of mine."

"He realizes now that he was wrong."

"Now's too late, Ma."

"It's never too late, son."

Chad didn't argue with his mother. He felt bad that she was caught in the middle, stuck with the thankless role of arbitrator. She never gave up trying to bring him and his father back together. He steered her away from that touchy subject once again by asking about all his sisters. They chatted amicably and said goodbye with promises to get together soon. Chad saw his mother as often as he could—at one of his sister's homes or when she visited San Francisco—but never at Sunny Hill Farm. And he sure had no intention of going back there for the old man's birthday party.

Chad's concentration had been poor enough before his mother's call, and now it was totally destroyed. He stuck the pile of invoices he'd been trying to sort out back in the desk drawer and thought about his father.

Chad had learned almost everything he knew about racehorses from him. King Barron was a master horseman and breeder. As a boy Chad worshipped him. Trouble was, the old man had demanded the same unquestioning worship when Chad became an adult. He ruled Sunny Hill Farm, passed down to him from his father and his grandfather before him, with autocratic disregard for the opinions of others, including his only son.

Chad recalled the intense struggle between them from the time he'd turned eighteen until he was twenty-one. By then he'd realized that he would have to leave his father's kingdom if he wanted to become his own man. Barron Senior had never forgiven him for that, and Chad had never forgiven his father for making it necessary.

Even now, over ten years later, anger coiled in Chad's chest when he remembered his last conversa-

tion with his father. Conversation, hell! It had been a
vituperative monologue delivered full blast by the old
man. The gist of it had been that if Chad deserted him
and the family business, he would be disowned.

Hadn't his father realized that threats would only
spur him to leave all the quicker? Chad believed he
had. He believed that his father had truly wanted him
to leave home so that he could remain the unchallenged ruler of his bluegrass kingdom.

Chad smiled grimly. The old man had gotten his
way as usual. He had Sunny Hill Farm all to himself
now. And Chad had his own business, one he'd strug-
gled to create out of nothing. If he didn't let up, if he
continued to drive himself as hard as a racehorse,
Chad knew he would eventually surpass his father's
accomplishments as a trainer and breeder. And the
best part was that, unlike his father, he would do it
completely on his own, without the aid of old family
money.

Chad looked down at the oriental rug beneath his
desk, the colors luminous in a pool of lamplight. The
rug was a Barron heirloom. His mother had sent it to
him when he'd been starting out as a trainer at Pacific
Downs. It came from his grandfather's study at Sunny
Hill, and Chad used to play on it as a child. The rug
was all he had and all he expected to get from his Barron forefathers. And that was fine with him. He
snapped off the desk lamp and left his drafty tack
room office.

The shed row was dimly lit and quiet, with only a
groom and a guard on duty. Chad took care to tread
softly, not wanting to disturb the nocturnal peace of
his easily excitable charges. He paused in front of Boy

Wonder's stall, the horse on which all his hopes and dreams were pinned.

"Hey, Boy," he whispered. "You're gonna become famous and win us the Triple Crown." The gray colt closed his eyes, seemingly unimpressed.

Chad moved on and as he passed Thunderbolt's stall he shook his head. He had no such high hopes for this fine-looking but recalcitrant beast. In fact, the only notable thing Thunder had managed to do since Chad had claimed him was bring Emily Holt into his life. And Chad didn't know whether to thank or blame Thunderbolt for that. If anyone could disrupt his life and interfere with his game plan, Emmie could. But he sure didn't intend to let that happen. He'd gone along with her idea of having a bothersome shareholders' meeting but he wasn't in any big hurry to call one. He had more important matters to deal with than one wrong-headed racehorse. But how long could he keep Emmie at bay, he wondered. More to the point, how long could he keep his growing desire for her at bay?

"You'd best forget about pretty fillies and concentrate on winning," Chad muttered to Thunderbolt. He decided to follow this advice himself.

A week passed without Emily hearing from Chad. He'd bamboozled her, she concluded, her heart heavy with disappointment. But if he thought he could stonewall her indefinitely, he had a surprise coming. She would contact Thunderbolt's other shareholders, herself, as she'd intended to do before Chad had so graciously offered to do it for her. What a fool she'd been to take him seriously!

When she got home from work Monday she called Florence Feducci first. Flo didn't sound too keen on the idea. "When I invested in Thunderbolt I was really putting my money down on his trainer," she told Emily. "Because Chad's a winner, he develops winning horses."

"Thunderbolt hasn't even finished a race, let alone won one," Emily pointed out.

"Some horses need more time to develop than others, Emily."

"But does Chad have enough time to give Thunder? Didn't Dr. Peterson say that he was overextending himself?"

"It's true Chad has doubled the size of his stable during the past few years," Flo conceded. "He's become the leading trainer at Pacific Downs."

"Good for him," Emily said dryly. "I only hope his personal ambition doesn't get in the way of my... I mean *our* horse's development, Flo. I'm not trying to cause trouble. I simply want to have a meeting with all the partners to discuss how Thunder is being handled. Chad himself agreed to it."

"He did? Well, that's different," Flo said. "When and where did he suggest we meet?"

"At his office," Emily replied. That was true enough. "As to when..." She hesitated. "Actually, Chad left that up to me to arrange." That was also true, Emily told her conscience. He'd left it up to her by default. "How about 6:00 p.m. tomorrow?"

Flo agreed and when Emily called Dr. Peterson and the other partner, Dan Watts, they also agreed after voicing their dissatisfaction with Thunderbolt's performance. The only partner left to call was Chad.

Emily paced in front of her telephone for a good ten minutes, trying to get up the nerve. It rang before she managed to. Her sixth sense told her who was calling.

She took a deep breath and answered in a steady voice that belied her fluttery heart.

"Hey, Emmie, this is Chad Barron. I called to set up that meeting we discussed."

Tell him you already did, Emily urged herself. But that would be akin to waving a red flag in front of a bull, not an easy thing to do. "I thought you'd forgotten," she said instead, stalling.

"No way. But things have been pretty hectic around here. Sorry about not getting back to you sooner, honey."

"That's all right." Emily couldn't believe she'd said that! She gave herself a mental kick in the shins for being so diffident.

"So what time do you want to get together?" Chad asked her.

"What about tomorrow at six?" She crossed her fingers.

"Why, that suits me fine," he said, genial as could be. "Would you mind calling the other partners about this, Emmie? Like I said, I'm pretty busy."

"I'd be happy to call them," she replied, feeling guilty about being such a dissembler. But why aggravate Chad unnecessarily? He had played right into her hands!

"Oh, by the way, Emmie," he said. "I have some news regarding Thunderbolt."

She tensed. "Not bad I hope."

"Well, you couldn't call it good. Seems the stewards don't take kindly to horses running the wrong way during a race. Late this afternoon I received official notice that Thunder has been banned from the track."

"Banned?" Emily repeated numbly.

"I can't enter him in any races for a month."

"That's not fair!" she protested.

"It's as fair as life gets," Chad replied. "And it could be worse. Like Flo said, let's just be thankful that it's bad behavior instead of a bad injury that's keeping him out of the running."

Emily agreed with that wholeheartedly. And then something Chad had slipped into the conversation clicked. "Flo? When did you tell Flo about Thunder?" she asked him in an edgy voice.

"Oh, ten minutes or so ago. I tried calling you first, honey. But your line was busy." He chuckled softly. "I reckon you were arranging your little meeting with Peterson and Watts."

"Flo told you."

"Yep. She assumed I already knew about it. Thanks for going behind my back like that, Emmie. See you in my office at six." And with that Chad hung up.

"I didn't go behind your back!" Emily shouted into the receiver even though the line had gone dead. She was furious with Chad for not giving her a chance to defend her actions.

Not that she had any reason to be defensive, Emily reminded herself. Even though he'd been insincere about it, Chad had consented to a meeting. And she felt totally justified in going around him, which was a lot different from going behind his back. The way Emily saw it, her father had bequeathed to her the responsibility for looking after his most cherished possession. She considered herself Thunderbolt's guardian. And if Chad resented her for looking after the horse's best interest, that was his problem, not hers.

After convincing herself that she had acted beyond reproach, Emily marched off to the bathroom to wash her hair. She figured it couldn't hurt to look her best while dealing with Chad tomorrow.

"I have far better things to do than sit around waiting for some horse trainer to put in an appearance," Dr. Peterson announced to the other three partners waiting in Chad's office. He was perched on the lumpy, cracked leather couch also occupied by Dan Watts, a short stocky man in a navy blazer and khaki slacks.

Watts checked his ostentatious gold watch. "It's six-thirty. Where the heck is he?"

"No doubt seeing to some horse or other," Flo Feducci said. She and Emily sat in canvas chairs in front of Chad's desk. "Horses don't seem to care what time it is."

"Neither does their trainer," Peterson muttered.

"I'm sure Chad has a good reason for being late," Emily said and then wondered why she had come to his defense.

But if Chad had a good reason, he didn't offer it when he strolled into the office a few minutes later. He plopped into his squeaky swivel chair, propped his feet on the desk, and smiled agreeably. His dark eyes glided from face to face and he gave each person a nod. All except Emily. He ignored her completely. "Looks like we're going to have us a little meeting, partners," he said in his lazy drawl. "Let's start off by you all doing the talking and me doing the listening."

No one said a word. They're all intimidated by Chad, Emily thought. Well, she certainly wasn't. At the same time, she didn't feel like speaking up first, either.

After a long, awkward minute, Chad lifted his eyebrows. "Maybe we should hold this meeting in Thunderbolt's stall so he could put in *his* two cents worth."

"That's about all that hay burner's worth!" Watts said, then laughed heartily to demonstrate that he'd been joking.

Emily cleared her throat. She didn't want any more time wasted on dead silence or dumb jokes. "Perhaps you should be the one to start off and tell us what you think Thunderbolt's problem is, Chad. After all, you're the expert, not us."

Chad looked at her for the first time and bowed formally. "How nice of you to acknowledge that, Miss Holt. But since this get-together was your idea, why don't you give us your thoughts on the matter first."

Put on the spot by him, Emily shifted uneasily. "Well, I do think Thunderbolt's racing behavior might improve with a stronger jockey." She looked around the room. "I'd like to know how the rest of you feel about that."

"I agree," Dr. Peterson spoke up. He smiled apologetically at Chad. "Not to disparage your charming fiancée."

His fiancée! Emily's ears began to burn. She hadn't realized that Jenny and Chad were *that* serious. But of course it made all the sense in the world that they should become a permanent couple. They shared a life-style.

"Whoa, Doc," Chad said. "Don't be getting me married before I'm good and ready. I'm not engaged to Miss Jessup. She's a friend. A professional friend."

Peterson sniffed. "According to your foreman, Moss, she's a lot more than that."

"You bet she is," Chad said, pinning the doctor with his dark flashing eyes. "She's one of the most competent jockeys at Pacific Downs. And I'm damn sick of having to defend her because she happens to be a woman." Chad turned his glare on Emily.

"You know very well that's not why I object to her," she told him.

"Well, that's why I do," Dan Watts put in. "I don't think a woman can handle a powerful racehorse."

"You don't?" Chad asked. "What about the women who come into your showroom to buy one of your overpriced sports cars, Watts? Do you tell them they can't handle the horsepower?"

"That's different. You don't need strength to handle *that* kind of power."

"No, you need skill," Chad said. "Like you do in a horse race. Jessup doesn't have to overpower a horse. She's got the talent to finesse it across the finish line. That usually works a lot better than trying to muscle down a thirteen hundred pound animal, believe me."

"Seeing's believing," Dr. Peterson said. "And I haven't seen Jessup manage Thunder very well."

"*No* jockey's managed to bring him in first. He's still a maiden," Chad reminded his partners. "The trainer I claimed him off didn't fare any better using a variety of male jocks." Chad extended his arms and opened his hands palms up. "I rest my case." Sure that he had proven it, too, he smiled.

How smug he is, Emily thought. "I say we vote on it," she suggested.

Chad's smile turned into a scowl. "Vote?" he repeated in a disbelieving tone as he stared at her.

She held her ground without flinching. "Why not? We're five partners with five equal shares."

"I second that suggestion," Peterson added.

"And I veto it," Chad responded. "That's not the way I run my stable."

Watts cleared his throat. "Legally we have the right. I checked it out with my lawyer before coming here today."

Chad swung his long legs off the desk. Legal or not, he'd be damned if he was going to have his power usurped by some two-bit investors who didn't know a damn thing about racehorses. He was about to stomp out and put an end to this ridiculous meeting when it occurred to him that if he did he would be reacting exactly like his father. He stayed put behind his desk.

"Okay. Have it your way, partners. We'll vote," he said calmly. He even managed another smile because he knew something they didn't. He'd been defending Jenny on principle only. After her last short-lived ride aboard Thunder, she'd told Chad that she would never race him again. There weren't many good jockeys at Pacific Downs who were willing to anymore. A horse like Thunder didn't help a jock's reputation.

He's taking this quite well, Emily thought, glancing at Chad. But she sensed that beneath his calm, easygoing manner there lay a volcano of volatile emotions that would erupt if he felt challenged or threatened. Apparently he felt neither at the moment.

"All those in favor of giving Jenny Jessup another chance with Thunderbolt raise their hands," Chad said, raising his.

He nodded approvingly at Flo when she lifted hers, clothed in a purple kid glove. Good old Flo. She hadn't said a word during the meeting, which was so unlike her. Chad interpreted this as silent support for him. They'd always gotten on. Flo knew her way around a racetrack, knew what to expect when she put money on horseflesh. Sometimes you win, sometimes you lose, but you never complain. It was the name of the game.

Emily, on the other hand, was a novice. A well-intentioned one, Chad believed, but all the good intentions in the world didn't stop her from being a nuisance. Most investors were, but they were a necessary evil if he wanted to continue to increase and upgrade his stock. The trick was to keep them from interfering too much. And the way to do that was by making their investments profitable. Thunderbolt wasn't cooperating in that department, though. So he would have to humor the people paying for his costly upkeep.

"Well, Flo, looks like we're outnumbered," he said amiably. "Jenny Jessup won't be riding Thunder anymore."

That had been far too easy, Emily thought. She instinctively knew that Chad was somehow stringing them along. But she could hardly object. He had given in to their demand...hadn't he?

"Do you have another jockey in mind to replace Ms. Jessup?" she asked.

"Replacing Jenny will take some doing," he replied. "But I've got plenty of time to find somebody willing and able." He looked at Peterson and Watts side by side on the couch and narrowed his eyes. Since when were those two so chummy? "You gentlemen haven't heard the latest development in Thunderbolt's saga, have you?''

"What happened now?" Watts asked.

"The stewards banned him from racing for a month," Chad said nonchalantly.

"A month!" Peterson sputtered. "We have to support that laggard for a month without any chance of winning a purse?"

"I've had it with that horse," Watts said. "I'd like to turn him in for a new model."

"He has deep psychological problems," Dr. Peterson declared.

A flicker of impatience passed across Chad's rugged features. "Let's not start analyzing Thunder, Doc. He's just a big randy colt who needs another year or so to settle down."

"A year or so!" Peterson looked at Watts, who looked dismayed. "A year of throwing good money after bad."

"You can't expect instant rewards when you invest in a racehorse. You're wagering on a career, not on a couple of races," Chad told them, not for the first time. He'd explained all this to them before taking their money and they'd assured him they were in for the long haul. But now that the glamour of owning a genuine racing Thoroughbred had worn off, and their friends were no doubt tired of hearing about it, they needed something else to brag about. Like having their horse *win* for a change.

"I haven't lost faith in Thunderbolt," Emily spoke up. "He's got the spirit to win and that's the important thing."

Chad grinned at her. He found her growing devotion to Thunder kind of sweet. Naive but sweet. How could he stay angry with Emmie when he knew that her heart was in the right place? What bothered Chad was that his own heart kept nudging its way closer to hers. He stopped smiling at her and looked at Peterson and Watts, who were murmuring together.

"We think we have a solution to Thunderbolt's problem," Peterson said to Chad.

"Do you now?" Chad's voice was soft, his eyes hard. When rank amateurs came up with proposals regarding his training program he could barely contain his impatience. But for better or worse, they were limited partners and deserved limited respect. "Let's hear it, Dr. Peterson."

"Obviously the horse needs his behavioral patterns readjusted," Peterson began.

Chad groaned softly. He didn't have time to sit and listen to psycho-babble. What was Peterson going to suggest—laying Thunder on the couch for a few sessions of therapy?

"Watts and I agree that gelding is in order," Peterson said.

Emily gasped. "Does that mean what I think it does?"

"It's a common procedure at racetracks," Peterson informed her coldly.

"It'll settle him down," Watts said, keeping his eyes averted from Emily's face. "I hear geldings tend to be more attentive."

"You're willing to disfigure that perfect animal on *hearsay?*" Emily turned to Chad, horror and desperation in her eyes. "Tell them, Chad. Tell them you will forbid such a thing."

"Forbid?" He attempted to look helpless. "But I don't have the right. As you've pointed out more than once to me, Miss Holt, this is a partnership. That's why you called this meeting in the first place, isn't it?''

"Don't worry, Emily. I'm not going to go along with the idea of turning Thunder into a soprano," Flo said. "I'm looking forward to being godmother to all the babies he'll eventually sire."

"Women! They sentimentalize everything," Watts grumbled.

"Baloney," Flo shot back. "I'm thinking of stud fees, mister. There's more than one way to make money on a Thoroughbred."

"If Thunder never wins a race he won't have any value as a sire," Peterson pointed out.

"Money? Is that all you people think about?" Emily asked in a disgusted tone.

"We're not as emotionally involved with this horse as you are, Ms. Holt," Dr. Peterson said. He looked away from her and spoke to the others in general. "This young woman has obviously transferred the love and devotion she missed giving her deceased father onto the horse he owned a share in. So naturally she's overreacting to the sensible suggestion that the stallion be gelded. You see, Ms. Holt has come to view Thunderbolt as much more than a mere horse. He's a symbol. When he loses his ability to reproduce it will be as if her father, the procreator of *her* life, had lost—"

"Put a lid on it, Doc," Chad interjected. He didn't know if the psychiatrist was spouting drivel or making sense. But he did know that the headshrinker's observations were an invasion of Emmie's privacy and he wouldn't abide that. "Let's just stick to the business at hand, okay? All those objecting to having Thunderbolt gelded raise their hands."

Flo reached for Emily's and they lifted their hands in a unified grip. Emily gave Chad a beseeching look but he didn't respond. He leaned back in his chair and folded his arms across his chest.

"And those in favor of it?" he asked.

Peterson's hand shot up, and Watts followed suit. Chad's arms remained folded.

"What's your vote?" Emily asked him in a barely audible voice.

Chad could tell she was close to tears. He couldn't bear to see her looking so miserable. "No," he said flatly. "We don't geld him."

Chapter Nine

The meeting broke up. Peterson and Watts departed disgruntled but resigned. Flo, satisfied with the outcome, bid Emily and Chad a cheery goodbye and left them alone in the office. Emily remained seated across the desk from Chad, eyes brimming with appreciation.

"Thank you for taking my side, Chad."

"There's nothing to thank me about." His tone was gruff. "I made a practical business decision. Your attachment to Thunder didn't influence me."

It gnawed at the back of Chad's mind that she *had* unduly influenced him, though. Peterson and Watts had been right to a point. If Thunderbolt continued his fractious behavior he would never win enough races to have any value as a sire. If gelded, he would probably be more attentive.

But Emily's horrified reaction to the suggestion had swayed Chad to her side, and he'd convinced himself that he could turn Thunderbolt into a winner by using less drastic measures. Would his decision have been the same if he hadn't found Emmie so touching in her distress? So downright appealing? Chad shifted uncomfortably in his chair. He wished she'd stop staring at him like that.

"I didn't assume I'd influenced you, Chad," she said. "I know you resent it when I interfere with the way you run things."

"Resent is a mighty harsh word," he hedged. "Let's just say I don't appreciate it."

"It won't happen again," she promised, standing up. "I'm willing to admit that calling this meeting was a bad idea."

Now that was more like it, Chad thought. He rose and walked around the desk to give her a friendly pat on the back. "No harm done, Emmie," he said magnanimously.

"Thank goodness! What heartless money grubbers Peterson and Watts turned out to be. Now I understand why you keep your investment partners at arm's length, Chad."

Trouble was, he wanted to do just the opposite with her. He wanted to put his arms around her slender body and press her close. Not that he had any intention of giving in to this urge. He meant to keep Emmie at a safe distance.

But then she looked at him with those big, concerned eyes again. "Oh, Chad, that talk about gelding Thunderbolt was so upsetting!"

"Don't worry, honey. I'll never go along with it," he said soothingly.

He hadn't intended to make a permanent commitment but her golden gaze mesmerized him. He felt himself being pulled into it, into the glowing vortex. He felt the warmth radiating from her and leaned closer and closer, inhaling her fresh, lemony scent as he captured her in his arms and buried his face in her hair. How good she felt to him as they melded together, thigh to thigh, chest to breast, a perfect fit. He wanted to hold her forever like this, in this moment of time. They swayed together, and in the background a Strauss waltz accompanied them. Chad's heart rose and dipped with the swelling music although his feet remained firmly planted on the ground. He would take nothing from her, he promised himself. He was simply comforting her.

The sound of footsteps made them both jerk back as if propelled apart by an explosive force. It was only Moss.

"I'm feeling heat," the foreman said as he stepped into the office. He looked from Chad to Emily, his craggy face blank. "In Boy Wonder's right front leg."

"Probably nothing serious," Chad said, his own expression deadpan. He and Moss had played poker together for years.

"Better come check anyways, Chad. Don't want Boy hurtin' when he races Sadday."

"Big stakes race Saturday. The Pacific Handicap," Chad explained to Emily. He looked back at Moss. "Aren't you going to say hello to Miss Holt?"

Apparently not. Moss merely nodded to her. "You coming, Chad?"

"I'll meet you at Boy's stall in a minute, Moss."

"Suit yourself." The old man shuffled out.

"Sorry about that," Chad said.

Sorry about *what,* Emily wondered. Hugging her with such unexpected tenderness? Or being interrupted? Or was Chad simply apologizing for his foreman's unfriendliness? Emily guessed that's what he meant.

"I didn't take it personally," she said.

"You didn't?" He ran his hand through his hair. "Well, good."

They glanced at each other confused, not sure what the other was referring to. It was always like this between them, Emily thought—a fleeting moment of sublime closeness followed by wary withdrawal on both sides. There seemed to be some kind of faulty current running between them that would cause them to connect, then disconnect. That's why her nerves always felt like frayed wire whenever she was around Chad. They had shared something special a moment ago—much more than a hug. Their hearts had touched. But now neither of them dared acknowledge it.

Chad cleared his throat. "Listen, Emmie..."

She held her breath, waiting for him to continue.

"I reckon I won't be seeing you around here for a while," he said. "Not until Thunder is allowed to race again, that is."

She got the hint and smiled bravely. "Don't worry, Chad. I'll stay out of your hair until then." Turning quickly to hide her disappointment, she headed down the shed row. Chad didn't call her back.

Emily had a date with Roger Molby the following Saturday. They planned to drive down the coast to Monterey Bay for lunch. Roger had been dying to show off his new sports car to her for weeks and she'd finally given in. As she dutifully admired the car from the curb she noticed the sticker on the rear bumper. Watts Imports. She pointed to it. "As in *Dan* Watts?" she asked Roger.

"That's right. He sold me this car personally. Do you know him?"

"I met him at a meeting the other evening. He owns a share of Thunderbolt."

"That racehorse you're so obsessed with?"

Emily laughed self-consciously. "Don't exaggerate, Roger."

"It's all you talk about, Emily. I was beginning to think Thunderbolt was a figment of your imagination."

"Oh, he's real enough. I couldn't possibly imagine a horse more beautiful."

Roger smiled indulgently. "He's probably a broken-down old nag."

Emily remained unruffled. She found Roger annoying at times but managed to overlook it. "If we didn't have plans to drive to Monterey I'd suggest going to Pacific Downs. Then you could see Thunderbolt for yourself."

"We can stop at the racetrack and then go to Monterey," he suggested.

Emily hesitated. Chad had practically ordered her to stay away. But didn't she have the right to visit Thunderbolt any time she pleased? Didn't she have a *duty*, as a conscientious owner, to check up on him? Of course she did. And if Chad Barron didn't like it, too bad!

"Let's go see my horse, Roger," she said in a determined voice. She folded herself into his fancy little car and slammed the door.

Roger winced. "There's no need to slam it so hard, Emily dear."

When they arrived at Pacific Downs Emily directed Roger to the private road leading to the back side. He was impressed when the gate guard greeted Emily by name and let them through.

"You must come here often for the guard to know you, Emily."

"Not that often." She smiled. "But I managed to make an impression on George one day."

She didn't go on to explain how, sensing that Roger wouldn't appreciate such audacious behavior. Chad had, though. She would never forget that look of admiration in his dark eyes when she'd breathlessly reached him after outrunning the guard. It was a look he usually reserved for his Thoroughbreds.

Roger parked in an area behind the barns. Emily jumped out and took a deep breath. "What a heavenly scent!" she exclaimed.

Roger wrinkled his nose. "Since when are you so crazy about the smell of manure, Emily?"

She laughed heartily. Roger was right. That was the prevalent scent. But there were so many others blending with it, combining to make an indescribable essence that only racetrack connoisseurs could fully appreciate. It occurred to Emily that she had become one of them. Less than a month ago she had been an outsider like Roger. But now she felt part of a whole new world. All thanks to her father, she thought. She was beginning to appreciate that he had willed her much more than a share in a horse.

She took Roger to Chad's barn, and the first person she saw coming down the shed row was Bobby Lee.

He beamed at her and tipped his cap. "I figured Chad would invite you, Miss Holt. You'll bring us luck for sure."

Emily had no idea what he was talking about.

Oblivious to her bewilderment, Bobby chattered on. "The big race isn't for another hour but I better go change. Chad wants me to look respectable when they take pictures in the winner's circle because Grandma will probably see our photo in the paper. That's how certain he is that Boy's going to win." Bobby tipped his cap again. "See you in the box a little later, Miss Holt. I'm real glad Chad asked you to come today." He hurried off without noticing her companion.

Roger eyed Emily suspiciously. "Isn't Chad the name of that cowboy I met in your office a couple of weeks ago?"

"He's not a cowboy. He's Thunderbolt's trainer."

"Why didn't you simply tell me you had a date with him instead of tricking me into bringing you here?"

"Don't be absurd, Roger. I don't have a date with Chad."

"That boy seemed to think you did," Roger persisted.

"Well, Bobby was wrong! Now let's go see Thunderbolt and then we can drive down to Monterey as we'd originally planned."

The backstretch had suddenly lost all its charm for Emily. She knew it was silly to feel hurt, but she couldn't help wishing that Chad had invited her to watch the big stakes race in his box.

Chad's stride was long on confidence as he headed toward his barn from the track kitchen across the road. A lot of well-wishers had come up to him during lunch to shake his hand, acting as if his horse had won the Handicap before he'd even run it. That's what a shoe-in they considered Boy Wonder to be around the backstretch.

But Chad wasn't going to let himself get all excited about it. Oh, no. He was going to stay calm and cool as usual, even though this particular race meant more to him than any other would all season. If Boy won the Pacific Handicap, he would qualify for the Kentucky Derby. And then there'd be no stopping that horse! Or his trainer.

Chad cautioned himself again to keep his cool. No sense setting himself up for disappointment. But he couldn't control his imagination from galloping full speed ahead, sprinting right past the race yet to be won today and on to the Kentucky Derby. He pictured his father watching from his special seat of honor at Churchill Downs, arms folded across his broad chest, a look of disapproval on his ruddy face. A look Chad knew all too well. Then he pictured the old man's eyes bulging with amazement as Boy Wonder crossed the finish line first. That's right, Pa! Boy Wonder—the colt that no-account son of yours bred and trained. How do you like them apples?

Chad laughed at himself. It wasn't like him to get so carried away. He'd better try concentrating on something else. Like Emmie Holt running. He'd been replaying that particular image for days now. Poetry in motion. He found the memory of her a lot more relaxing than her actual presence. Emmie had far too disturbing an influence on him in the flesh. The more he saw of her, the more he wanted her.

But Chad didn't *want* to want her. The last thing he needed right now was to get sidetracked by a woman.

Too many other things needed his attention. Like his forty-some Thoroughbreds in various stages of condition from tip-top to crippled. And his transient staff of grooms and handlers in various stages of competence from expert to inexperienced. And his many investors in various stages of meddling from mildly pesky to royal pains in the butt. No, there was no room on his agenda for a passionate affair right now. Not that Emmie seemed inclined in that direction herself. She didn't strike Chad as the sort of woman who would get swept away by passion.

When he reached his barn Chad immediately noticed a stranger sitting on a wooden bench at the far end. Chad didn't like strangers on his turf. There were too many snoops and touts slithering around the back side, looking for a hot tip or good horse to claim away.

"Hey you," he called, walking toward the man. "What's your business here?"

Roger immediately stood up and brushed off his designer jeans. "Why, I'm here with Emily. She introduced us a few weeks back if you recall."

"Right." Chad gave him the once-over with narrowed eyes. "Name's Moby, right?"

"Molby," Roger corrected. "Emily told me to wait here while she went looking for you."

Chad's sharp gaze wandered up and down the barn, searching for her. Knowing that Emily was around caused his heart to beat a little faster, the way it did during a horse race. His face remained an expressionless mask when he spotted her coming out of his office. Her green knit dress, cinched with gold at the waist, accentuated her long supple limbs as she hurried toward him. Chad loved watching her move.

"Where's Thunderbolt?" she demanded in lieu of a greeting when she reached Chad.

"In his stall munching hay I reckon." He smiled at her.

"He's not! There's another horse in his stall."

Chad shammed surprise. "Are you sure, honey?"

"Of course I'm sure," she replied impatiently. "Do you think I don't know my own horse?"

"They all look more or less alike to me," Roger said. Both Chad and Emily ignored him.

"Did you come to wish me well today, Emmie?"

"No." She looked away from Chad and then back at him. "I mean, of course I wish you well. I hope Boy wins the Handicap for you. But I came to see Thunder, not you."

"Well, since you're already here, why don't you stay for the race?"

"You could have invited me earlier," she pointed out, sounding more petulant than she'd intended to.

"I didn't think you'd be interested in watching any horse run except Thunder. He's the only one you care about."

"That's not true. I check the form charts every day to see how the horses from your stable performed, Chad."

"Do you really?" Chad's wide mouth eased into a bemused smile. "Well, how about that. I'm touched."

Roger cleared his throat. "Let's not waste much more time here, Emily dear. We have a fairly long drive ahead of us."

She turned to Roger and frowned slightly, as if not quite remembering who he was or why he was standing there. "Of course," she said vaguely and looked back at Chad. "So where have you hidden Thunderbolt?" she asked him.

"It's pretty hard to hide a half ton of hot-blooded flesh and muscle, honey," Chad replied. Almost as hard as hiding his growing feelings for *her,* he silently added.

"Well, you seemed to have managed to do just that," she said.

"I moved Thunder to a stall on the other side of the barn," Chad told her. "As far away from Rosie as I could get him. I figure he'll settle down better without that filly driving him to distraction."

"Poor Thunder." Emily laughed. "He's in love."

Chad didn't find it the least bit amusing. "He's in lust, not love," he said brusquely. "Come on. I'll show you where I've put the randy son of a gun."

They began walking down the aisle together. Then Emily remembered Roger and turned around. "Aren't you coming with us?" she asked him.

Roger looked sullen. "Only if you want me to, Emily."

She felt a stab of guilt, realizing that she'd been ignoring him. Chad certainly had the power to make other men pale by comparison, she thought wryly. Roger had become invisible!

"Of course I want you to see Thunderbolt," she said, offering Roger a warm, conciliatory smile. "That's the whole reason we came here in the first place."

"Is it?" he muttered. But he fell into step with her and Chad.

The moment Thunderbolt caught sight of Emily, he extended his powerful neck over the stall door and nickered his greeting. Emily went up to the colt and rubbed her arm under his throat. She'd completely lost her fear of him the day she'd bathed him.

"Here he is in the flesh, Roger. What do you think of him?" she asked proudly.

"A very nice animal indeed," he replied stiffly, keeping his distance.

"Nice? Why, he's beautiful!" Emily kissed Thunder's muzzle.

"Must you do that?" Roger asked in a disgusted tone.

"Don't be jealous, Molby. You can kiss him, too, if you'd like," Chad said.

"You're not as amusing as you think you are, Barron." Roger looked at Emily. "Thank you for showing me your horse. Shall we go now?"

"But we just got here." Emily pressed her cheek against Thunderbolt's neck and inhaled his rich scent.

"What's your rush, Molby?" Chad asked in a friendly tone. "Why don't you and Emily stick around for Boy Wonder's race?"

"Horse racing bores me," Roger replied. "It may be called the sport of kings but I consider it the folly of fools."

"To each his own," Chad replied genially, ignoring the insult. "But this is the most important race of the year at Pacific Downs. Some of the finest horses in the country are competing in it. The purse is considerable."

"Chad's horse stands a good chance of winning," Emily put in. "Isn't that exciting?"

Roger stifled a yawn or perhaps only pretended to. "We can listen to the race on the radio on our way to Monterey if you'd like, Emily. Now if you're through fondling that big brute, let's go please."

"Emily, you don't have to leave if you don't want to," Chad said evenly.

But she felt that she did. "I promised Roger I'd spend the day with him," she said and gave Thunderbolt a fond farewell pat.

"Why don't you let Emily off the hook, sport?" Chad suggested to Roger. "She obviously wants to stay."

Was it that obvious? Emily wondered. She hoped not. She knew how sensitive Roger was and didn't want to hurt his feelings. Thunderbolt had no such qualms it seemed. He extended his neck and gave Roger a hard shove with his nose.

"Hey!" Roger shouted, barely maintaining his balance. He quickly backed away from the horse's stall.

"He was just being friendly," Emily said but she wasn't so sure about that.

Chad chuckled. "Amazing how horses can read minds."

Roger looked at the horse trainer warily, then turned to Emily. "I'd like to talk to you alone for a moment."

"I'll be in my office," Chad said. He strolled off whistling to himself.

Roger watched Emily watching Chad walk away and sighed. "I thought you were obsessed with the horse but now I realize it's the trainer you're crazy about."

"What?" Emily tore her eyes from Chad's retreating form and stared at Roger, genuinely surprised by his remark. "You don't know what you're talking about."

"I know that you never look at me the way you look at *him*."

Emily couldn't refute that. When she looked at Roger she saw an attractive enough man but he didn't affect her equilibrium in the slightest. The moment Chad came in sight her blood raced. But she certainly wasn't obsessed with him!

"Not that I have any right to be jealous," Roger continued. "You've never led me on, Emily. Even so, I hoped I could persuade you to consider me more than a friend. Until today, that is." Glancing at Thunderbolt, he smiled with resignation. "I guess I needed a good shove to make me see the light." He turned back to Emily and offered his hand. "Goodbye, dear. I've never been one to fight a losing battle."

Left speechless by Roger's little speech, Emily accepted his hand. Perhaps, some day in the future, they could be friends again, but Emily sensed that he didn't want to hear her make that offer now. So she said nothing at all. Instead, she pressed his hand between both of hers and then let go. She let him go with the heartfelt hope that he would find a woman who would love him. Without another word he turned away and walked out of the barn. And out of her life.

Emily heard his sports car start up, and as the sound of the motor receded it occurred to her that Roger had left her stranded. She wasn't upset by her predicament, however. She felt at home in the barn and could think of no place she would rather be at the moment.

She scratched Thunderbolt under his ear and talked nonsense to him for a while, and then went to find Chad. She didn't know how she was going to explain Roger's departure to him, but she certainly didn't intend to mention that Roger had accused her of being obsessed with him.

It was so absurd, Emily thought as she headed for Chad's office. Granted she often dreamed about him. Granted she often thought about him during her waking hours, also. But that could hardly be termed an obsession. She simply wasn't the type of woman who became fixated on a man.

But when Emily stepped into Chad's office, all reasoning drained from her head as her heart did a somersault. Chad stood with his back to her, naked from above his low-riding jeans.

She attempted to clear her tight throat but couldn't quite manage it as she marveled at his beautiful proportions. His arms and back were all sinewy muscles, sleek and tan. Yet there was an elegance in his brawny physique and a certain vulnerability to his nakedness. Emily almost felt like a Peeping Tom as her eyes swept over his torso.

He turned, as if sensing her presence although she hadn't so much as breathed.

"Oh, there you are," he said casually. He tossed the denim work shirt he held onto his cluttered desk.

His chest was as hairy as his back was sleek and Emily's blood ran hot through her veins. She also felt it rush to her cheeks. "Excuse me," she managed around her thick tongue. "I didn't mean to interrupt you."

"Interrupt what?" Chad flashed his grin. "I'm just changing shirts for the Handicap. Have to fit the image of a champion Thoroughbred owner when they hand me the trophy in the winner's circle."

Chad's unflappable confidence thrilled Emily almost as much as his bare chest did. She watched as he took a folded white dress shirt from his desk drawer and ripped off the dry cleaner's band encircling it.

"Too much starch," he muttered as he shook out the shirt. He slipped it on and grimaced. "If there's one thing I can't stand, it's too damn much starch."

He's nervous, Emily realized. Her observation was confirmed as she watched him fumble with the buttons. This moved her even more than his outward confidence had. Her heart did a little tap dance as it went out to him.

"Here, let me help you," she said as he impatiently attempted to work one of the small cuff buttons into its stiff hole.

He extended his arm and Emily bent her head, giving the simple task her intense concentration. She was all thumbs—trembling thumbs. The intimacy of the moment disquieted her. But that didn't stop her from boldly reaching up and fastening his tiny collar buttons. The scent of him, a mixture of shirt starch, soap and heady masculine musk, made her a little dizzy. When she'd fastened the buttons she stepped back to regain her sense of balance.

"Nothing like a woman's touch," Chad said.

"Aren't you going to ask me where Roger is?"

"I don't really care just so long as he's gone, Emmie. I spotted right off that he wasn't the man for you. And you saw that for yourself today when ole Thunder gave him the heave-ho. So you followed suit."

"I did no such thing. Actually, Roger was the one who decided he was wasting his time with me."

Chad considered this a moment. "Then he never bedded you," he stated flatly.

Emily forced a laugh. "What makes you so sure?"

"No man in his right mind would decide to give you up after making love with you, Emmie."

His deep-set eyes seemed to penetrate to her soul. "What makes you so sure?" she asked again. But there was no bravado in her voice now.

He didn't answer her. Instead, he broke their intense gaze and looked around the room in an abstracted manner. "Now where the hell is my tie?"

He put a great deal of energy into searching for it, rummaging through the clutter on top of his desk, yanking drawers open and banging them shut, then searching the top of his desk again.

Emily found his tie for him, hanging on a wall peg in the middle of a row of reins and bridles. It was a beautiful tie, dark blue silk embossed with tiny gold horses. She handed it to him.

"I was just getting my hopes up that it was lost for good," he said. "Nothing I hate more than wearing a neck noose."

"It won't strangle you," Emily assured him. "But now you're going to have to undo your collar buttons."

"That's okay. You can do them up for me again."

Emily watched him tie his tie with jerky but sure movements, the silk making a raspy sound as it glided through his rough palms. She was surprised when he managed a perfect knot. Perhaps he wasn't as unpolished as he liked to pretend he was. The tie, she had noted, came from Cable Car Clothiers, one of San Francisco's finest men's stores, and his broadcloth shirt had his initials monogrammed in pale grey on one cuff.

"All set. You can button me down again, Emmie," he said.

She went through the same painstaking procedure all over again, frowning and biting her full lower lip as she maneuvered the tiny buttons into the collar openings. But this time, when she was done, Chad captured her hands by the wrists and kissed each palm lightly before releasing them.

"Thank you," he said.

Emily, taken aback by the gentleness of his gesture, only nodded.

"Pardon me," he then said. He abruptly turned his back to her and unzipped his jeans. The sound of the zipper seemed to run down her spine. He stuffed his shirt tails into his pants, zipped up again, and notched his thick leather belt with the horse head buckle. He turned back and spread open his arms. "Well, do I look halfway presentable now, Emmie?"

She could not recall ever seeing a more handsome man, except for a vague memory of her father in a seersucker suit and Panama hat, his "lucky track clothes." Recalling this bothered her, and her tone was sharp when she replied. "You could use a haircut."

"Yep, I reckon I could," Chad agreed, running his fingers through his thick black crest. "Never got around to it this month."

"You look fine," Emily assured him, regretting her criticism. But she couldn't resist reaching up to smooth down the hair his fingers had ruffled. He allowed her the liberty, even bowing his head to convenience her effort to tame his shaggy locks. His hair felt coarse and vibrant beneath her hand. The texture delighted her and even after she lowered her hand she felt a tingling sensation on her palm.

"You look mighty fine yourself," Chad told her. He slowly took her in from head to foot, and Emily held her breath under his examination. "Light over the kidney," he said. "I like that."

She laughed nervously. "Is that another horse term?"

He nodded. "That's what we call one that's slender loined. Not that I'm comparing you to a filly, mind you. It's just the way I tend to express myself. I meant no offense."

"No offense taken," Emily said. And then it bubbled out of her, something she had no intention of ever confessing to him. "Sometimes I dream that you're a horse. A centaur, actually."

"Well, I'll be damned." He tossed back his head and roared.

Blood rushed to Emily's face, and she squirmed under the heat of her blush. She wanted to kick herself for telling him that. And if he didn't stop laughing, she was going to kick *him*.

He did stop, only to give her a sly, teasing smile. "Emmie, Emmie, Emmie," he drawled, shaking his head. "You are full of surprises, honey. That's about the sexiest thing any woman ever said to me."

She opened her mouth to protest, to make it clear that the dream was hardly as erotic as he was making it out to be, when a sonorous voice boomed over the track loudspeaker.

"Trainers, bring your horses to the paddock for the fifth race, the Pacific Downs Handicap."

Chad's amused expression evaporated, to be replaced by a taut mask. He took a deep breath. "This is it, Emmie. The big one."

She forgot all about her embarrassment as she absorbed the tension emanating from him. "I didn't realize how important this race was to you until now, Chad."

"Important?" He ran his hand through his hair, mussing it up again. "It's *everything,* Emmie. I would sell my soul to the devil to win it."

"You don't mean that."

"Well, I'd surely be tempted to. The purse is so large that it would stake my future in this business." His dark eyes looked beyond her and toward a private vision. "I could breed my own champions, then. I could train them right from the start instead of relying on claimers that other trainers have practically ruined. I would give up almost anything to have that chance."

"You shouldn't stake your future on something as risky as a horse race, Chad." Emily hated risks herself. She always played it safe and sure.

His lips stretched into a smile. "I do it every day, honey. My business is always on the line—the finish line. That's why I love it so much. I'm addicted to living on the edge." He plucked his buckskin jacket off a wall peg and shrugged into it. "Would you like to come to the paddock with me while I saddle Boy Wonder? Or we could meet in my box."

"I'll wait for you there," Emily replied, sensing that Chad wanted to devote his complete attention to his horse before the race.

"Wish me good luck again, Emmie," he said. "But on the lips this time."

Emily stood on tip-toe and kissed him softly.

"Once more for good measure," he commanded.

So she did it again.

"This could get to be a habit," he said. He lowered his head and kissed her back. It was a hard, firm, no-nonsense sort of kiss. It was the kiss of a man who expected victory. He released her and grinned.

"You're my lucky charm, Emmie," he declared and left the office.

His lucky charm. The words echoed in Emily's heart as a deep warmth enveloped her. She couldn't understand why she was so deeply affected by them. And then she suddenly did understand, and a chill replaced the warmth. That's what her father used to call her. His lucky charm!

All the warning signals in Emily's system went off. Chad had so many traits in common with her father. Not only physical attributes—the dark thick hair, the strong build, the soft deep voice—but Chad was also a gambling man. His life centered around the racing game just as her father's had. The only difference was that her father had gambled from the front side and Chad did it from the back side.

From the first moment she had laid eyes on him, Emily had sensed that Chad was a danger to her. She'd instinctively known that he was the one man who could hurt her as deeply as her father had. Not that he would ever deliberately do so. Now that she'd gotten to know Chad better, she appreciated that he had a gentle nature beneath his obstinate exterior. But her father had never deliberately set out to hurt her, either. He'd simply found the lure of the racetrack irresistible. He'd given her up for *that*.

And so would Chad Barron. Only moments before, he had declared that he would give up almost anything—even his soul—for the intoxicating thrill of horse racing. It wasn't a sport to him. It was his very reason for existence.

That's why she could never allow herself to fall in love with him no matter how strong the attraction.

Sure that her good sense would take control of her wayward emotions, Emily proceeded to the clubhouse. She would watch the race with detachment and then take a taxi home.

Chapter Ten

About a half-dozen people had already gathered in Chad's box when Emily arrived. They greeted her as if they knew her, and it took Emily a moment to realize that they were members of Chad's crew. She hadn't recognized them at first because they'd dressed up for the occasion. Even Moss! He stood by the rail, his sparse gray hair still damp from a shower and his craggy face so freshly shaven that his chin still sported a dab of shaving cream. He wore pressed blue jeans, a Western shirt and a string tie with a horseshoe slide.

"Afternoon, Miss Holt," he said, his tone as close to affable as she'd ever heard it. "Fine day for a race, ain't it?"

But even as he made this observation a mass of clouds began crowding out the sunshine.

"Yes, a very fine day," Emily said, ignoring the sudden overcast. She wanted to support Moss in his uncharacteristic effort to be positive. "Chad invited me to watch the Handicap from here," she added, just in case the foreman assumed she was intruding.

"Figured as much," Moss said.

A silence followed, and Emily racked her brain to come up with a way to continue this rare conversation with the taciturn foreman. She didn't want to ask any questions about the upcoming race, sure that Moss would be impatient with her ignorance. Perhaps not, though. He seemed different to her today. He certainly smelled different. As she stood by Moss she got a whiff of intoxicating men's cologne.

"I invited a lady friend myself," he finally said.

Doing her best to suppress her amazement, Emily was about to ask him who the lucky lady was. But then she heard a familiar voice call out.

"Yoo-hoo. Here I am, Moss!"

Will wonders ever cease? Emily asked herself as she turned to greet Flo Feducci.

Flo looked delighted to see Emily. "Can't stay away from the track, can you, sweetie?" she joked. "You're turning into a real rail bird. Like father, like daughter." Her expression changed to one of consternation. "Oops. That was a dumb crack to make. Sorry."

"Don't be." Emily knew that she had meant well and changed the subject to put them both at ease. "Your hat is charming," she told Flo. And so it was— a concoction of artificial violets and tulle.

"Purple is my favorite color," Moss put in. His unexpected declaration caused both women to stare at him. "Well, it *is,* dammit," he growled. "And I've always been partial to women who wear it."

"In your own sour way you're kinda sweet, Mossie," Flo said, slapping him on the back.

Mossie? Emily managed to control a giggle by concentrating on the infield tote board. Boy Wonder's current odds were one to two. "Looks like Chad's horse is the favorite," she said.

"So was Thunderbolt the time he refused to leave the gate," Flo reminded her.

"Yeah, but this time the bettors are right on the money," Moss stated. "Boy is the strongest runner in the field beyond a shadow of a doubt and should come in first."

"Why, Moss, I've never heard you be so optimistic before," Flo remarked. "Are you sure you're feeling all right?"

"I didn't say he'd win," the foreman grumbled. "I just said he *should* win. There ain't no such thing as a sure thing."

"Except for death and taxes," Flo said cheerfully. "Who's steering Boy today, by the way?"

"Budenberry again. Chad was considering asking that Jessup gal but listen to this…" Moss paused and leaned toward the two women. "She up and flew off to Vegas this weekend with that young vet, Doc Revera. They're gonna get hitched there." He shook his head in wonder. "And all this time I thought she was settin' her cap for Chad."

"I knew you were wrong about that," Flo said.

"I expect I was," Moss admitted reluctantly. "But I'm right when I say that women and horses don't mix. You either devote yourself to one or the other. Just ask my three ex-wives."

"Three!" Flo looked more impressed than shocked. "Why, Mossie, I never imagined you to be such a lover boy." She gave him a poke in the arm and he made a barking sound.

The sound of Moss actually laughing, Emily mused. She decided that it was time to leave him and Flo alone and moved farther down the rail without them even noticing. Hearing the news about Jenny Jessup getting married had set her heart soaring for a brief moment, until she reminded herself that it shouldn't matter to her. What difference did it make that Chad and Jenny weren't romantically involved? Absolutely none, Emily silently insisted. And yet she still felt a surge of relief that she couldn't control.

She noticed that the horses were being led out to the track for the post parade, which meant that Chad would be coming to the box soon. Sure enough, she heard members of his crew call out his name a moment later and looked back to see him shaking hands with everyone. The sight of him caused her wayward heart to start soaring again. Emily reined it in as he made his way toward her.

"Did everything go all right in the paddock?" she asked Chad politely when he reached her.

"Couldn't have gone better," he replied. "Boy's really pumped up for this race."

Emily could tell that Chad was also pumped up, although he looked outwardly calm as he casually leaned against the rail, a pair of binoculars hanging from a strap around his neck. But his eyes glittered with excitement when he looked at her. He couldn't fool her.

The loudspeaker crackled. *"Three minutes to post time."*

Chad curled his big hand around Emily's as they watched the horses file past. His palm felt dry and warm against hers, and she marveled at how secure and relaxed it made her feel to hold hands with him. They seemed to be alone in the crowd.

"There's our Boy," he said when the gray colt passed their box.

Emily gazed up at Chad's rugged profile as he watched his horse. He looked so proud, so confident, so absolutely in charge of his destiny. Yet she had sensed his nervousness in the barn, and as she studied him now she could see his pulse throb at his temple. She could almost hear his heart pounding.

"One minute to post time."

She squeezed his hand. Because this Handicap race mattered so much to him, she realized that she couldn't view it as objectively as she'd intended to.

"They're at the post!"

She even said a little prayer for him.

He grinned at her. "I'm so glad you're here beside me, Emmie."

She hoped he wouldn't call her his lucky charm again. He didn't. He released her hand and raised the binoculars to his eyes to watch the horses being loaded. The back gates to the stalls slammed shut, one by one. Seconds after the last horse was in the bell clanged and the front gates flew open.

"AND THEY'RE OFF!"

As Chad followed the race through his binoculars, Emily did her best to sort out the confusion. All twelve horses were bunched together.

"Dammit, he can't break through," Chad muttered.

Emily managed to spot Boy Wonder then, caught behind four other horses.

"Go wide, go wide," Chad said softly, as if he had a direct pipeline to the horse's ear. "Thataboy, thataboy, now you can set the pace. Go ahead, go ahead, go ahead." She heard Chad suck in his breath as his horse took the first turn, and then hiss an expletive.

"What's wrong?" she asked.

He didn't reply. Emily doubted that he'd even heard her. He was totally connected with his horse. And she was totally connected with Chad, watching him instead of the race. The race didn't matter to her. Only his reaction to it did. But he showed so little. He didn't move a muscle and his eyes remained hidden by the binoculars. In two minutes it was all over. Chad lowered his binoculars and looked at her. His face was an impassive mask. The light had gone out of his eyes. He said nothing.

The announcer cried out the winner. It wasn't Boy Wonder. He didn't even place or show.

No one in the box approached Chad. None of his crew said a word to him. They drifted off, as silent as if they had just attended a funeral. Even Moss stayed away. He gave Chad a brief salute and then left with Flo. Emily and Chad stood alone, she looking at him, he staring out at the track.

Emily wanted to wrap her arms around him and hold him close. She ached to comfort him but sensed it would be the wrong thing to do.

"Boy never had a chance to set the pace the way he likes to do," Chad finally said. He shrugged. "There's only one way to win but a thousand ways to lose. Oh, well. Just another day at the races."

It was that indifferent shrug that did Emily in. "Don't pretend it doesn't matter!" she cried.

"It's not the last race that matters, Emmie. It's the next one. Look. They're already preparing the track for it."

But she wouldn't look away from him. She had to say it before the words choked in her throat. "Oh, Chad, I'm so sorry Boy didn't win for you."

Chad gently chucked her under the chin. "You can't let it get to you like that, honey. It's business."

She could tell the loss had upset him, though. He was pale beneath his tan, and she'd never seen him look so exhausted. She longed to stroke his face and soothe away his disappointment. But it wasn't her place to comfort him. She had no place at all in his world or in his heart. And that, Emily reminded herself, was the way she wanted to keep it.

But oh, how vulnerable he looked to her now—like a little lost boy trying to put up a brave front. She could feel her heart tugging in his direction.

"Chad, you look beat," she told him, then regretted her choice of words. "I mean tired. Why don't you call it quits for the day and go home?" It occurred to Emily that she had no idea where he lived or how he existed away from the track. For all she knew he slept in the barn with his horses! But then she remembered that he'd mentioned owning a ranch.

"You're right," he said. "I've had enough of this place for today. Bobby Lee will see to Boy. I left him at the paddock ready to lead Boy to the winner's circle." Chad laughed hollowly. "I even made the poor kid put on a *tie* for the pictures." He yanked his off impatiently and threw it down.

"Chad! That beautiful tie."

"It's unlucky. I don't want it anymore."

A superstitious, disappointed, headstrong little boy, Emily thought. This made her want to smile for some reason. She picked up his tie and shook it out. "Go home," she suggested again.

"You come with me," he commanded.

"Oh, no, I don't think that would—"

"Please, Emmie. I don't feel like being alone right now."

And she didn't feel that it would be wise to be alone with him. His vulnerability made her feel vulnerable, too. But how could she refuse him? Still, she hesitated.

"Please, Emmie," he said again. "Come home with me and I'll show you my new baby."

Emily's mouth dropped. "Your baby?"

"Dropped just last week. Sweetest foal you ever did see. Likes to nibble on your fingers."

That did it. Emily's resistance cracked wide open. "I'd love to see your baby, Chad," she said.

The sky became more and more overcast as Chad and Emily drove out to his ranch, thirty miles north of Pacific Downs.

"I haven't done much to prettify the place," he said as they went down a bumpy dirt road marked Private. "I don't usually invite people up here. In fact, I never do."

Emily couldn't help but be pleased at hearing this. It made her feel special. And Chad's ranch didn't need "prettifying" as far as she could see. It looked so picturesque to her. The road was lined on either side with white plank fences and emerald pastures, and soon they passed a well-maintained red barn. They traveled a few hundred yards farther up the road and reached a simple redwood ranch house.

"Home sweet home," Chad said, parking his Jeep in front of it. "I got steaks in the freezer and beer in the fridge so we're all set for a nice long evening ahead.''

Were they? Emily gave Chad a wary sidelong glance. She'd agreed to see his foal, not have dinner and spend a *long* evening with him.

"I don't want to get back to the city very late tonight," she said primly.

"Why? Do you turn into a pumpkin at midnight?"

"It's the coach that turns into a pumpkin, not the princess, Chad. Men never seem to get those things straight.''

"But I got your message straight, princess. You don't intend to spend the night with me." He hopped out of the Jeep. "Don't worry. I hadn't intended to ask you to."

Knowing she should feel relieved, Emily felt slightly offended instead. Didn't Chad find her sexy enough? That doubt was erased when he opened the car door for her and watched her get out. His glittering eyes devoured her legs. And it thrilled her.

They went inside his small house and he turned on a floor lamp in the living room. It was only late afternoon but the sky had become so dark that it could have been twilight.

"Well, what do you think? I decorated it myself," he said tongue in cheek.

Emily had to laugh. The room was sparsely furnished with a plaid sofa, a rocking chair, a TV perched on a wagon wheel coffee table, and the wrought iron floor lamp. No curtains on the windows. No rug on the floor.

"The minimalist school of decorating," she remarked.

She moved to the one point of interest in the room— a long wall shelf crowded with horse racing trophies and framed photographs of various women on horseback. "That's quite a collection," she said, referring to the pictures rather than the trophies. Chad's taste seemed to run to the same type, dark-haired beauties who sat tall in the saddle.

Without the least encouragement from her, Chad pointed to each of the photos and named the woman depicted in an affectionate tone. "That's cute Katie. And beautiful Beth. And Sue Ellen. I call her Sukey. And Sweet Sandy. And darlin' De De. Sukey's my favorite. I see her the most. Of course I love them all. I make it a point to keep up a relationship with each and every one of them."

Bully for you, Emily thought. "Relationships with five women must keep you pretty busy," she remarked dryly.

"Not to mention their families," Chad added. "Those gals have given me fourteen terrific nieces and nephews."

Realizing that the women in the photos were Chad's *sisters,* Emily smiled with relief. "What about your parents? Do you have any pictures of them?"

"Mom's camera shy. It's become a joke in our family, how she disappears the minute she spots a camera. We kid her about being a secret agent or something."

"And your father? Is he camera shy, too?"

Chad laughed sharply. "No way. He glories in being in the limelight. And he sure as heck doesn't want to share it with anybody." Chad's tone was light but Emily picked up the trace of bitterness underlying his words. He immediately changed the subject. "You still want to see my foal, don't you?"

"Of course! That's why I'm here."

"No, it isn't," Chad said. He gently tilted up her chin and stared into her eyes. "Admit it, Emmie."

"Admit what?" The words almost stuck in her throat.

"You're here because you feel sorry for me."

Was that all? She didn't say anything.

"And don't think I don't appreciate it, honey." He gave her a quick kiss on the forehead.

The sort of kiss he would give one of his sisters, Emily thought. She once again felt disappointment. What was wrong with her anyway? She shouldn't even have come here, let alone be disappointed that Chad was acting the perfect gentleman.

"I better take out those steaks," he said.

She followed him into the small neat kitchen. He pulled two steaks from the freezer and placed them on the counter.

"Care for a beer?" he asked her.

It wasn't Emily's favorite beverage. "No thanks, but you go ahead and have one."

"Later. Why don't we go out to the barn?"

They left by the back door and Emily looked up at the threatening sky. "The storm's going to break any minute now," she said. "I love a good hard rain storm. It's such a powerful release of energy."

"I could use a release myself right now," Chad said. "Race you to the barn, Emmie?"

"You're on!" She knew the value of a good head start and sprinted ahead across the pasture.

Chad stayed behind, captivated by the sight of Emily's tight buttocks moving rhythmically beneath her

clinging knit dress. And then he realized that he was
letting her get too far ahead. He took off after her and
had to push to catch up. She was even faster than he'd
reckoned. He would have to strain to beat her. Instead, he held himself back. Let her win, Chad told
himself. Let Emmie feel that rush of winning again.

She was delighted when she reached the barn door
before he did. Delighted and breathless and flushed.
She leaned against it, laughing and gasping. "I'm out
of shape," she said.

"No, you're not, honey. You're in fine shape." Her
shape was as fine as they came, he thought.

She took a deep breath. "I can't believe I actually
beat you."

"Hey, you don't have to rub it in." He shammed
annoyance. "After all, I was never an Olympic
champ."

"Neither was I."

"You could have been."

"Oh, Chad." Emily shook her head. "You don't
know that."

"Yes, I do," he insisted. "Don't you think I can
spot a champion runner when I see one? That's how I
make my living, honey. If you were a horse I would
give up everything I owned to claim you."

Emily laughed. "I'll take that as a compliment."

"That's the spirit it was given, Emmie."

He really could be so dear, she thought. He could
say things that made her heart sing. "You let me win,
didn't you, Chad?"

"No way."

"You *did,*" she insisted and reached up to ruffle his
hair.

He tossed back his head like a playful stallion. "Are you accusing me of throwing a race?"

"You bet I am, mister. I'm going to report you to the track officials."

"Those are fighting words, honey."

"Oh, yeah?" She mussed up his hair some more. "So what are you going to do about it?"

He grabbed her wrist and yanked her closer. They both started breathing hard again. But not from exercise this time. Their eyes locked. Their lips parted. And then Chad released his grip and stepped away.

"We'd better get inside before we get drenched."

"But it hasn't even started raining yet."

"Let's not tempt fate," he muttered, swinging open the barn door.

How right he was, Emily thought.

The barn was cool and dim and smelled sweetly of hay. Chad led the way past some empty box stalls. The mare and her foal were in the last one.

"Hey, Gemini. I brought a visitor to see the little guy," he said softly to the dam. She accepted this news calmly as her baby nursed.

Emily leaned over the Dutch door to get a good look at the foal. His head was tucked under his mother's flank as he suckled. Dam and foal were the same mahogany shade.

"His legs are almost as long as those of a full-grown horse," Emily commented.

"Mother Nature designed them that way because foals have to keep up with their dams in the wild," Chad told her. "Less than fifteen minutes after this one was born he was standing. Within twenty-four hours he could gallop."

"Amazing," Emily said. "Doesn't he get restless in a stall all day?"

"He and Gemini are turned out into the open paddock every morning. A neighbor takes care of them while I'm away."

"The mother is beautiful."

"Gem's a champ in her own right. A good brood mare is more important than the stallion in my opinion. She influences the offspring a lot more."

That he should say this surprised Emily. "I thought breeders cared more about the sire."

"You can have your overpriced studs. Give me a mare that carries well and has the right disposition any day," Chad replied. "Heck, even the quality of her milk has a bearing on the foal's future."

A dreamy smile tilted Emily's lips as she listened to Chad's deep soft voice and watched the foal nurse. She sighed deeply. She felt content and relaxed and at peace with the world. Being around animals did that to you, she supposed.

She realized that Chad had stopped talking and wondered how long she'd been daydreaming. She looked up at him. He was staring at her with an intensity that shattered her calm mood. Her heartbeat became agitated as she recognized his look was one of pure desire. She heard the rumble of thunder in the distance.

"Sounds like it's coming closer," she said.

He nodded. "Luckily, thunderstorms don't bother Gem. Some horses get jumpy, but not her."

Emily felt plenty jumpy, though. And it had nothing to do with the weather. "I think it's time you drove me home, Chad."

"Don't you want to stay for dinner?"

"Those steaks will take hours to defrost. Why don't we have dinner at a restaurant in town?"

"Whatever you say, Emmie." His manner was off-hand, as if it made no difference to him.

They walked to the barn door, neither of them speaking. Emily had never felt so at odds with herself. How could she want Chad so much and yet be so afraid to want him? And what about Chad? How could he look at her with avid desire one moment, and then turn away from her so easily the next? Why couldn't human needs be *simple,* she wondered.

And in the next moment everything did become simple and basic and as natural as rain. As Chad threw open the barn door a super discharge of lightning ripped through the sky, accompanied by a deafening clap of thunder. Both Emily and Chad jumped back and automatically clung to each other.

"Wow, that was a big one," Chad said in awe.

Emily shuddered. "I've never experienced anything like it." The air was charged with electricity. The light hairs on her forearms tingled.

And then the rain began streaming down in torrents. It was as if a pitchfork had snagged a long tear in the heavy clouds.

"Want to make a run for it?" Chad asked.

"I don't want to run anymore," Emily answered softly.

"Neither do I." He pressed her closer against him, and she could feel the heat of him. "I've never wanted a woman more than I want you right now, Emmie. Do you feel the same?"

She couldn't speak. She nodded.

But that wasn't good enough for him. He gripped her upper arms and turned her to him so he could look

her full in the face. "Tell me, Emily Holt. Tell me you
want me, too."

"Yes," she whispered. "I have from the beginning."

"Me, too. You're always on my mind. It drives me
crazy."

"I think I'm going crazy, too," she admitted.

"If I kiss you now I won't be able to stop. Not this
time."

She gazed into his deep dark eyes. The dreamy smile
had returned to her lips. "So kiss me. I won't ask you
to stop."

He lowered his head, slowly, slowly, and every
molecule in her body seemed to pull toward him until
their lips met. Oh, the sweet relief! She had been
yearning for another kiss from him for far too long.
She opened her mouth to him. His taste was sublime.
And while they kissed the lightning crackled in the
open doorway, illuminating them. Igniting them.

He pulled her away from the door and shut it, still
keeping a hold of her with one hand. As if she'd bolt
away from him. As if! She had committed herself to
him now—totally and completely.

He led her to an empty stall, carpeted with a layer
of fresh straw. "Don't move," he commanded and let
go of her wrist.

He slipped off his jacket and spread it over the
straw. Then he unbuttoned his shirt, his movements
unrushed, his eyes never leaving her face. He removed it and spread it out on the straw, too. "Now I'll
undress you," he told her.

He unclasped her gold belt. It fell to the ground,
soundlessly sinking into the straw. He pulled her little
knit dress over her head and threw it aside. It was

useless to both of them now. He gazed at her in her panties and bra and smiled with satisfaction. "I like lace," he said. "Those can stay on for a little while longer."

He took his sweet time getting to know her body in detail. She had guessed that his lovemaking would be slow and deliberate, sensual and gentle. She had seen him glide his big hands over horses to gentle them, to soothe them. His hands. His big magical hands. They were all over her, stroking, kneading, fondling her flesh.

And all the time he was kissing her and she was kissing him back. Madly. They stood ankle-deep in straw, exploring each other. His thigh pushed against her legs. She parted them and gripped tightly. She rubbed against him, the lace of her bra catching against the hair on his chest.

"Time for this to go," he said, unsnapping the front of her bra to reveal her small round breasts. "Ahh," he sighed. "I love 'em."

Emily threw back her head and laughed. He was a man of few words and always to the point. He kissed her exposed neck, then stopped to arrange her tangles of russet curls around her bare shoulders. He took great care doing this, as if it were the most important thing in the world to get the arrangement right.

"There," he said, stepping back. He tilted his head and narrowed his eyes to study her, standing before him bare-breasted and bold, her nipples taut and her chest rising and falling with the knowledge that she was about to become his. *His!* "Oh, Emmie, how lovely you are."

She soaked in his admiration and had no shyness with him. She wanted him to look at her. She wanted to reveal herself to him completely. All her fears and doubts seemed to have been washed away by the heavy rain. It pelted the barn roof, a sharp, staccato beat that matched the beat of her heart.

He knelt before her and slid down her panties. He held her hand as she stepped out of her shoes, and then her underwear. Hay stuck to the soles of her feet. He kissed her flat belly and his hot breath tickled. He circled her navel with his tongue. She shivered with delight.

"Are you cold?" he asked, looking up at her.

She buried her hand in his hair and pressed his cheek against her abdomen. "I'm burning up," she said.

He stood to tower over her again and cupped her buttocks. "Perfect conformation," he pronounced. "Lie down for me now."

She complied. It was what she wanted. Beneath his shirt and jacket, the hay felt soft and spongy. She watched as he unbuckled his horsehead belt and unzipped his jeans. Then, for the first time, he hesitated. "I just remembered your dream about the centaur," he said. "I don't want to disappoint you, Emmie, but I'm just a man. All man."

"Yes, you certainly are," she agreed when he took off his jeans and briefs. She glanced up to the rafters and smiled her appreciation. "And I'm *not* disappointed."

He had the legs of a horseman, slightly bowed, the thighs lean and muscular. His body was fit and trim from the physical work he did day in and day out. Yes, Emily thought, he was a fine example of the human male animal—powerful yet touching in his nakedness.

"My darling Chad," she whispered.

He lay down beside her on the straw, and held her to him. Flesh to flesh, they pressed together, imprinting themselves upon each other—her pliant breasts molded into his solid chest, his male part contoured against her thigh. They held each other a long time, as if to make up for all the times they had kept their distance and avoided touching. Now they touched completely, from their lips to their toes.

He began stroking her again, his roughened palm light across the rounded planes of her hips and buttocks. She kissed his shoulder, his neck, his ear. When she slid her tongue along the velvety skin behind his ear he groaned with pleasure.

He became more intense in his lovemaking then, more demanding. It was as if she had pressed some secret button that released his control. He threw her back and took the tip of her breast in his mouth, sucking deeply, pulling her desire to the surface. She cried out with an aching pleasure and he laughed softly. His hand roamed between her thighs, to the moist warm center of her.

"Yes," he said in his low quiet voice. "You do want me, Emily Holt. And I can't wait to have you any longer." He lay back and pulled her on top of him. "I don't want the straw to scratch your delicate hide," he said, grinning up at her.

He had given her control, Emily realized. If he were the steed, then she was the jockey. As she moved above him, she watched his reaction. It was wonderful to see how deeply she affected him, how responsive he was to every nuance of her movements. She became centered on him, filled with his masculine power. But she was the one who found a rhythm and set the pace. Her breasts bounced up and down as they raced faster and faster together, traveling through time and the inner realms of sensual pleasure. His face and chest glistened with sweat as she pushed him to the limit, and she gasped as she stayed with him, feeling wild and free. She could never harness this passion. She didn't even try. They cried out in unison as they crossed the finish line together . . . both of them winners.

They gazed at each other with stunned expressions, then Chad drew her to him, to lie across his chest. They lay still and breathless for a long time, listening to the rain together, listening to each other's heart beat.

"Wow, that was a big one," Chad finally said.

Emily smiled, recalling that his remark had been the same after the enormous thunderbolt. "I've never experienced anything like it," she replied, also recalling her response earlier. Every conversation they'd ever had was etched in her mind.

They laughed softly together, enjoying their little private joke. They would share many more, Emily thought. Their capability to share both physical and mental intimacy seemed endless to her at that moment. She fitted her cheek against the slope of his shoulder and readjusted her body atop his into a more comfortable alignment of soft flesh and hard muscle.

He chuckled, pressing up against her. "Oh, my sweet Emmie," he said. "You won't give this poor man a chance to catch his breath before making him want you all over again, will you?''

His immediate responsiveness to her slightest movements delighted Emily. Realizing that his powerful desire for her had given *her* such power shook her to the roots.

''I love you, Chad.''

The words slipped out without her considering them. Perhaps, if she had thought about it, she would have been more guarded with her feelings. But she didn't regret telling him the truth any more than she regretted making love with him. Sometimes life was a gamble, she thought. Sometimes you had to stick your neck out and take risks. It was the first time in her life that Emily had ever believed this. Love had made her more brave, more open than she'd considered herself capable of being. What a gift this man had given her!

But he took it away in the next moment. He didn't say a word or move a muscle but she felt a change in him. A pulling back. Their bodies and minds had melded so completely that she now understood every nuance of the big, silent man beneath her.

''What's wrong?'' she asked in a small, apprehensive voice. She no longer felt so brave.

''Nothing, Emmie. You're wonderful,'' he responded in a thick voice. He stroked her hair, gliding his fingers through her tangle of curls without pulling them.

How gentle he could be, Emily thought, but she sensed that his caress was abstract, a calming gesture while his mind roamed away from hers.

''Tell me, Chad. What's wrong?'' she asked again.

She already knew the answer, however. She had confessed a love he didn't share with her. Her heart shattered into a thousand pieces.

"We have to talk," he said. And his firm voice made it clear to her that all her apprehensions were valid.

Chapter Eleven

Emily rolled away from Chad and stood up. As she sifted through the hay for her undergarments, she felt awkward and ridiculous.

"If it makes you feel more comfortable, forget that I said I loved you, Chad," she suggested, gritting her teeth so hard that she was sure the molars would crack. What a hopeless fool she was!

Chad reached out and grabbed her ankle. "Whoa there, honey. You've got no call to be upset."

She pulled her ankle from his clasp. "And you've got no reason to be concerned. I'm not going to try to pressure you into a commitment or anything, Chad. If I love you that's my problem, not yours." Tears stung the edges of her eyes, but she was sure she could contain them. She kicked around the straw. She'd feel much better, she knew, if she could just find her clothes.

Chad got up and brushed stalks off his body. He scooped up his shirt and handed it to Emily. "Here, put this on before you get cold," he said.

Without thanking him, incapable of uttering the words, she slipped into it and rolled up the sleeves. She couldn't look at him now.

"Listen, Emmie. The thing is—" he sighed deeply "—I love you, too."

Emily did look at him then, eyes wide. His tone had been so doleful that she wasn't sure she'd heard him correctly. "You love me?"

"Yep. But falling in love wasn't part of my game plan. I don't have *time* for it, dammit."

She wondered if he knew how ridiculous he sounded. It didn't matter. All that mattered to her at the moment was that he loved her. She knew he wasn't just saying it to make her feel better. His expression may have been troubled, his tone gruff, but love light emanated from his eyes. The shattered pieces of her heart melted together again to form a throbbing whole.

"Don't you worry, darling," she told him. "I'm an independent woman, not a clinging vine. I won't monopolize your time. I have my own demanding career and my own life and—"

"People in my neck of the woods get married when they're in love," he interrupted. "They settle down and start a family."

She'd forgotten what an old-fashioned man he was. She smiled gently. "Let's take it one small step at a time, Chad."

"I'd say we took a pretty big step a little while ago, Emmie." Now he was the one who looked offended. And started looking for his own clothes. He gave up finding his briefs and pulled his jeans over his nakedness. "I sowed my wild oats a long time ago," he told her. "I'm not lookin' to do that anymore."

"Neither am I!" she protested. "I don't go around having meaningless affairs if that's what you're implying, Chad Barron."

"I'm not implying that at all. Don't you think I know what kind of woman you are, Emily Holt? *You* are the woman I want in my life, lady. For good and always. But the racetrack has always come first with me, and I'm afraid I'll let you down like your father did."

Emily froze. He had voiced her deepest fear. "Will you abandon me in the end, too, Chad?" she asked in a barely audible voice.

"Not physically, honey." He immediately took her into his arms and held her tight. "But maybe you'll feel emotionally abandoned by me because of my work."

She couldn't believe that was possible—not while he was holding her against him with such fervor. Every joint, every muscle, every vein in her body thawed in the heat emanating from him.

"I've got a driving ambition," Chad continued. "One that's probably in overdrive. And meeting up with you was like an enormous roadblock I hadn't expected." He stepped back to look her in the eye. "I reckon what I'm trying to say is that I don't want love to detour me, Emmie. I'm too committed to breeding and training the best racehorses possible to commit myself to marriage now."

"You're the one who keeps bringing up marriage, not me," she reminded him gently.

"Well, it's heavy on my mind," he grumbled. "I always imagined proposing to the woman who made me feel the way you do."

In truth, Emily had always imagined it that way, too. But she'd learned the hard way that life wasn't as smooth and perfect as that. There were *always* road-blocks and unexpected detours. Knowing this made her feel a little wiser than Chad at that moment. She smiled up at him, a soft smile with a tinge of sadness in it.

"It's enough to love each other right now, isn't it, Chad?"

"It's more than enough," he replied. "It's something to treasure." He kissed her with supreme gentleness, but when he gazed at her again the desire in his eyes was sharp and hard. "Come on, Emmie. There's a big comfortable bed waiting at the house for us."

She arched an eyebrow. "It seems ambition isn't the only thing you have in overdrive, Chad Barron."

He laughed heartily and scooped her up in his long, strong arms. He carried her back to the house in the pouring rain. It took them less than two minutes to shuck off what little they were wearing and dry each other off. They didn't want to keep that big bed waiting.

When had she ever been happier? Never, Emily decided as she arranged a bouquet of cornflowers and daisies at Chad's kitchen table the following Friday. She had brought the flowers with her after work, along with a bag of groceries, her overnight bag and her cat. Chad had given her the key to his place and told her to make herself at home. He'd promised that he would leave the track early to join her, and she looked forward to a romantic weekend together.

Emily stepped back to admire her arrangement. Adding this feminine touch really did make her feel more at home. She wondered if Chad would ever consider putting curtains on the windows. A bold stripe in the kitchen would be nice. Perhaps muslin in the living room. Nothing lacy or ruffly or overdone, of course. Chad wouldn't care for that. Watch it, she cautioned herself. He asked you to spend the weekend with him, not redecorate.

Emily had resolved to live for the moment, not worry about what lay down the road with Chad. All she knew for sure was that she adored being with him, making love with him, sharing a part of his life. She began unpacking the groceries. It was nice to have someone to cook for, she thought.

By nine o'clock that evening Emily's high spirits had deflated somewhat. Chad hadn't returned from Pacific Downs yet, and the pork tenderloin she'd prepared was drying out in the oven. He'd phoned an hour earlier to tell her that a sick horse in his stable had taken a turn for the worse, and he had to wait for the vet. Emily had been genuinely sympathetic and understanding.

The phone rang again, and Emily hoped Chad was calling to say he was on his way, not that he would be even later. But when she answered, a woman responded.

"Oh, my, did I dial the wrong number? Is this Chad Barron's residence?"

"Yes, it is," Emily said. "But he isn't here now. May I take a message?"

"You could tell him to call his mother once in a while." Mrs. Barron laughed. "Not really. Chadwick is pretty good about keeping in touch with me. Do you know when he'll be home?"

"I really couldn't tell you, Mrs. Barron. He's dealing with a sick horse right now. You could try reaching him at the barn."

"Oh, I won't bother him. Would you think it presumptuous of me to ask who *you* are? I'm not used to hearing a female voice answer when I call my son's home."

That piece of information delighted Emily. She told Mrs. Barron her name. "I'm here...uh...making dinner for Chad," she said.

"How kind of you. You sound like a very nice young lady, Emily. Have you known my son long?"

Emily smiled over the gentle third degree she was getting. "Long enough to think he's pretty terrific, Mrs. Barron," she replied.

"Well, well. That does sound promising. But I won't push my luck and ask you any more personal questions. Would you do me a little favor, though, Emily? Would you remind Chad that his father's birthday party is coming up?"

"Sure," she said. It seemed a simple enough request.

When Chad came home, he found Emily asleep on the sofa, her cat curled up in her lap. He turned off the TV and sat beside her. The cat sprang up and scurried out of the room, but Emily remained undisturbed. Chad kissed her on the cheek and she opened her eyes.

"I'm sorry I'm so late, honey," he said.

"What time is it?"

"Past midnight." Chad wrapped his arm around her. "I'm sorry," he said again. "But I warned you about my work. It never really ends."

She placed her head on his shoulder and breathed in the scent of horses and man. "I'm not complaining," she murmured sleepily.

"Not yet you're not. But you might get good and sick of my erratic hours soon enough. You'll come to the conclusion that I'm not worth waiting for."

Emily wished he wouldn't make their relationship sound so temporary and snuggled against him. "How's the horse?"

"He's going to make it."

"Thank goodness."

Chad sighed and buried his face in her hair. "Lord, it feels good to have you back in my arms. Now that I'm home, what would you like to do, Emmie?" He nibbled her neck. "Watch some more TV?"

"Mmm, no."

He cupped her breast with his big, warm palm. "How about a game of checkers?"

"Mmm, no."

"We could read in bed."

"Mmm, we could do that, I suppose," she said lazily. "But I have a better idea of what we could do in bed." She whispered it in his ear.

"Why, you wanton hussy," he said, shamming shock. He picked her up and carried her toward the bedroom.

"Are you hungry?" she asked as they went through the kitchen.

"I'm ravenous, honey. But not for food." He shifted her in his arms.

"That's good. Because dinner's ruined."

"Our evening together isn't, though." Chad placed her on the bed and proceeded to prove that to her all night long.

Emily awoke at sunrise to the sound of Chad singing in the shower—his own unique version of opera with gibberish for words and many off-key notes. If it hadn't been the man she loved who was singing, she would have covered her head with a pillow. But because Chad was the one producing the racket, the sound was truly music to her ears.

But why so early in the morning? She hoped that he intended to come back to bed with her. He padded into the room with a towel wrapped around his middle, his thick black hair slicked back.

"Up and at 'em, partner!" he bellowed.

Emily found his vigor amazing considering his lack of sleep and the amount of energy he'd expended the night before. She smiled, her toes curling up with pleasure at the memory of it. "You're joking. The sun's not even up yet."

"Best time of day, Emmie. Come out to the barn with me while I feed Gemini."

Emily groaned. He wasn't joking. "Chad, it's the weekend. Don't you ever relax?"

He looked at her puzzled, as if she'd suggested some unheard of practice. "This is what I do every day," he said. "But you take it easy, honey. I'll even serve you breakfast in bed before I go to the track."

She sat up and covered her breasts with the sheet. "You're going to the track *today?*"

"Just for a little while. I want to check up on that sick horse and make sure everything's under control.

I'll be back before noon and we'll have the whole day together, Emmie. We'll do anything you want.''

What she wanted was for him to stay with her. ''Can't Moss or Bobby handle things for one day? Why do you always have to be there?''

''Because it's my job to be there,'' he explained simply and patiently. ''Three hundred and sixty-five days of the year.''

''Well, I'm not going to hang around here all morning waiting for you to come back,'' she declared, throwing off the covers and getting out of bed.

His face tightened. ''You got sick and tired of me a lot sooner than I thought you would, Emmie.'' His voice was low and pained as he looked at her lovely body.

''Don't be silly.'' She went up on her bare toes to kiss him. ''I'm going to the track *with* you, darling. I'll visit with Thunder while you do whatever you have to do.'' Smiling at the relief in his face, she brushed past him and headed for the bathroom.

Chad pulled back the curtain while she was in the shower shampooing her hair. ''Mind if I join you?''

''But you just had a shower.''

''I'm up for another one,'' he said, untying the towel wrapped around his waist.

She looked down at his nakedness and laughed. ''So I see.'' She let him in.

They arrived at the racetrack a little later than Chad had planned to, but since the cause of the delay had been so pleasurable, he didn't complain about it. He was pleased that Emily had accompanied him. He wanted to share his world with her now. He liked the way she looked dressed in jeans, running shoes and a simple blue cotton shirt. He always liked the way she looked in clothes. Almost as much as the way she looked without them.

"You warm enough?" he asked her as they walked to his stable. There was a chill in the early-morning air.

"I'm fine," she assured him. He put his arm around her for warmth, anyway. "I forgot to tell you," she said. "Your mother called last night."

Chad laughed. "I bet she was surprised when you answered the phone."

"She said as much. We had a short but pleasant conversation. She told me to remind you to come to your father's birthday party."

"Boy, she'll use every trick in the book to try and get me there," Chad muttered.

"Doesn't sound as if you plan on going."

"You can bet your bottom dollar I'm not."

"Why not?"

"Let's not ruin this gorgeous morning discussing my old man, Emmie."

Inside his barn, the grooms were mucking out the stalls. Chad greeted each one by name and wished them good-morning. The horses had already been fed their breakfast, and after checking on his sick horse, Chad made his rounds from stall to stall with Emily.

"The first thing I look at is the feed tubs," he told her. "If a horse isn't eating, I know something's wrong. What I want to see is all the tubs licked clean. That's a sight that warms a trainer's heart."

When they reached Thunderbolt's stall Chad could tell the sight of him warmed Emily's heart, and he became concerned about her growing attachment to the horse. It simply wasn't wise. He had warned her about this already, however, and said nothing more about it as she petted Thunder. He moved on to check the rest of his charges.

Emily caught up with him as he was taking the bandages off the legs of a horse that had run the day before, to examine him for signs of soreness.

"I feel a little heat in the back leg," he told Emily. "Let's go see if he's nodding."

"What's that mean?" Emily asked.

"If a horse has a lame front leg, his head will come up when the sore foot hits the ground," Chad explained. "If it's his back leg that's bothering him, his head will go down when the sore foot hits. That's called nodding off."

Chad put a shank on the horse and led him out to the side road to jog him. Emily came along and ran beside them.

"His head's going down!" she said after observing the horse intensely.

Chad, who had spotted that right off, smiled to himself. She was so earnest and eager to help. Yes, he was glad she'd come with him.

They returned to the barn and went to his office. Moss and Bobby Lee and some of the exercise riders were already there, waiting for Chad to give them instructions. He checked the blackboard hanging behind his desk, which he used to keep track of all the horses, then told the riders which ones he wanted galloped or breezed or jogged. Nobody paid much attention to Emily, which made her feel right at home. They listened to Chad and then left to do what he wanted done.

Chad poured Emily some coffee. "Not the most romantic way to spend Saturday morning, is it?" He didn't wait for her reply. "As soon as I see to a few more things, we'll get out of here, honey."

She laughed at that.

"Emmie, that's a promise. How about some fancy restaurant for lunch? Would you like that?"

"Oh, Chad." She reached up and brushed back a stray lock of his hair. "I can go to a fancy restaurant with anybody. I don't care about that. Hanging around the backstretch with you is a lot more fun."

"You really mean that, don't you?" He took back her coffee cup, placed it on his desk and hugged her close. "You make me very happy, Emily Holt."

Moss ambled in, as if on cue. "You gonna supervise the workout today or not, Chad?"

He reluctantly released Emily. "Lucky you weren't born a horse, Moss, because you've got real bad timing," he grumbled.

"Can't a body ask a simple question around here without getting his head bit off?" Moss grumbled back.

"Go ahead," Emily urged Chad. "I'll be fine."

"But what will you do to pass the time?"

"I think I'll go for a drive," she said. "Could I borrow your Jeep?"

"Sure," Chad tossed her the keys. "Any place special in mind?"

"Yes," she said, but she didn't tell him where.

Emily drove to the cemetery overlooking Pacific Downs Racetrack. It was small, and after a brief search she found her father's simple tombstone. She had delayed coming here for weeks, afraid of the powerful emotions it would call up, but now all she felt was a numbing sadness.

Emily believed that she had finally gone beyond the pain and insecurity his desertion had caused her. For all these years she had been unable to love or trust a man because of her father's rejection, but Chad had changed that. She couldn't help loving him, and because she loved him she had no choice but to trust him completely. She had convinced herself that Chad would never hurt her as her father had. He would never betray her trust.

Love softened Emily, and she could no longer be angry with Edmund Holt. She knelt at his grave and said a prayer for him.

As she drove back to the track, Emily felt at peace with her father. Her memories of him were vague but warm, and he would always be part of her present because of Thunderbolt. Thunderbolt! Emily smiled. The horse meant even more to her now because it had brought her and Chad together.

"I have great news," Chad announced when Emily returned to the barn and found him alone in his office. "The stewards have agreed to lift the ban on Thunder because the racing secretary is desperate to fill the seventh race tomorrow. Thunder meets all the qualifications. The purse is twenty thousand dollars and the field is weak. He can win it, Emmie! I know he can do it."

Chad's confidence in Thunderbolt thrilled Emily more than the chance of winning the purse did. But then misgivings began to surface. "Will he break all right this time, Chad? What if he doesn't?"

Chad shrugged off her concern. "I've been working Thunder at the practice gate and he's been doing fine. We can't coddle him, Emmie."

"You're right. We've got to let him go for it."

"That's the spirit, honey." But his smile wavered a bit and it seemed as if he were about to tell her something more.

"What is it, Chad?"

"Nothing. I was just thinking that we should get out of here right now. I want some time alone with my gal. You name it, Emmie. Any place you want to go."

"Back to your ranch?"

"Yes," he said, gazing at her with longing. "We'll go home."

He hurried her down the shed row. When a groom tried to detain him with a question, he told him to go ask Moss. They hopped into the Jeep and drove away without looking back.

"This is the first time I've ever left the backstretch in the middle of the day," Chad said.

"How does it feel?" Emily asked him.

"Kinda strange," he admitted. "But I've got to learn to let go a little bit. You've made me realize that, honey. There's more to life than my work." He paused. "There's *you*."

His simple declaration filled her with warmth. She had never felt so close to a man before. Chad had become part of her, and she wondered if she could ever separate herself from him again. She dared hope that she would never have to.

"You're so quiet, Emmie. What are you thinking about?"

"You and me. How good it is together."

"It's the best," he replied thickly. "I'll never get enough of making love to you."

She hadn't been talking about sex. Chad was right—it was the best—but she'd meant much more than that.

She didn't tell him that, though. He would have to come to understand it himself. And it seemed that he was beginning to. He had left the backstretch behind to be alone with her, hadn't he?

"Mind telling me where you went for a drive earlier?" he asked her.

"I visited my father's grave."

"Ah, so that's why you're so pensive. Would you like to talk about him with me, Emmie?"

She touched Chad's hand to show that she appreciated his offer. "There's not much to say, really. I was so young when he left. I don't even know if what I remember about him is true or a little girl's wishful thinking. What about your father, Chad?"

"King Barron? Oh, you don't want to hear about him." Chad shifted into fourth and drove faster.

But Emily did want to hear about him. She wanted to know everything she could about Chad. "Your father's name is King?"

"Yep. That's what he's known as, anyway. He claims people started calling him King because he's the top horse breeder in Kentucky, but I think he gave himself that nickname. His real name is Chadwick."

"Oh, so you're Barron Junior."

Chad grimaced. "That's what the old man used to call me. Junior. I couldn't abide it."

Emily couldn't imagine anyone daring to call Chad "Junior," even his own father. "Tell me what he's like," she asked again.

"I don't rightly know," Chad said after a moment. "My father changed on me. I idolized him growing up. He was everything I wanted to be... an expert horseman, strong and patient and hardworking. Devoted to his family, too. And loyal to his friends. But then I had the audacity to disagree with him about the way I wanted to live my own life, and he turned into a hard-headed, intolerant dictator. Needless to say, we had us a parting of the ways. I didn't want to be like him anymore."

But you are! Emily almost cried out. Didn't Chad realize that he could have been describing his own good and bad traits? Obviously he didn't, and he wouldn't appreciate having her point it out to him, either.

"You inherited your father's skill with horses," she remarked mildly instead.

"That's in the Barron blood for sure," Chad allowed. "But I sure as hell didn't want to spend my life under his control. He predicted my complete failure when I went out on my own. And I've dedicated my every waking hour to proving him wrong."

"Then you're still under his control," Emily said softly.

"What?" Chad turned his eyes from the road to look at her sharply.

Emily didn't repeat her observation. She knew Chad had heard her loud and clear.

"If you're gonna hang around with me, Emmie, you'd better learn one thing real quick," he said.

Her heart sank. He was going to tell her to learn to mind her own business. "What's that, Chad?" she asked anyway, raising her chin.

"How to ride, honey," he replied, surprising her once again. "No Barron worth his weight in corn falls in love with a woman who can't ride alongside him. I'd like to start teaching you on my Appaloosa. If you take to it we can get you a horse of your own. How does that sound?"

Her heart soared once again. "It sounds wonderful, Chad!"

He chuckled. "Is this the same gal who came into my life awhile back declaring she had no use for horses and would never get on one?"

"People change when they fall in love."

"Do you think I have, Emmie?"

She smiled, taking in his blunt, stubborn profile. "You're beginning to, darling. You're beginning to."

When they arrived at the ranch the wall phone started ringing the minute they stepped inside the kitchen.

"Damn. That's probably Bobby or Moss calling about something that can probably wait until tomorrow," Chad said.

"I'll answer," Emily offered. "If it's not an emergency I'll say you can't be disturbed."

He grinned, eyes glittering. "Tell 'em I'm going to spend the rest of the day and night making passionate love to the most beautiful woman in the world."

"I certainly will not!" She smiled back. "But hold that thought." She picked up the receiver and said hello.

"Is this Emily Holt?"

"Why, yes." She didn't recognize the voice on the other end.

"My wife mentioned she spoke with you last night. Is Junior there? Uh, I mean Chad."

"One moment, please. I'll see." She pressed the receiver to her breast. "Chad!" she whispered. "It's your father!"

"My father?" he boomed back. "That can't be."

"Shh. It *is*. Talk to him." She held out the receiver to him.

He shook his head vehemently.

She shook the receiver at him.

He walked out the back door.

"I'm sorry, Mr. Barron. He's not available at the moment."

"I reckoned he wouldn't be, but my wife convinced me to give it a try." Mr. Barron's voice sounded weary and resigned. "You tell him something for me, will you please, Miss Holt? You tell my boy I'm sorry." And with that he hung up.

Emily went outside to find Chad on the back porch, looking out toward the open pasture.

"That was unbelievably rude, Chad," she said in a shaky voice. "And cruel."

He kept his back to her. "You don't know anything about it, Emmie."

"That's true, but it seems I've been made the go-between. Chad, look at me, please. I have a message from your father."

He turned to face her, his expression impassive.

"'You tell my boy I'm sorry.' Those were his exact words."

Chad didn't so much as blink. Or respond.

"Doesn't that mean anything to you, Chad?" Emily's voice cracked. "I always longed to hear my father say that he was sorry to me. Just once."

"But King didn't say it to *me,* Emmie. If I had spoken to him he probably would have told me to go to hell again."

"He didn't call to tell you that! Oh, Chad, he made the first step. That's the hardest one. All you have to do is call him back. Do it. Right now."

"There's no rush," he said grimly. "We haven't spoken for ten years. I'm real sorry he put you in the middle of this, honey. But I don't want to discuss it."

Emily sighed. "All right." It made no sense to argue in his father's behalf. She was on Chad's side, after all. She would always take his side. "Let's talk about something else," she suggested.

"Like how lovely you are?" He reached out to run his fingers through her hair.

She smiled, glad his good humor had returned, glad they were back to touching again. She pressed her cheek to his shoulder. "Tell me more about Thunder's race tomorrow."

She felt him stiffen slightly. "I told you everything already."

"No, you didn't." She pulled away to look at him. "You're holding something back, Chad. I sensed that in your office, too."

"I just didn't want to worry you unnecessarily. It happens to be a claiming race but that—"

"A claiming race!"

"But that doesn't mean anyone's going to claim Thunder," Chad continued in a calm tone. "Who would want to? He's got two bad races on his forms and a reputation for being a refuser."

"But you said he stands an excellent chance of winning this race."

"He does. But nobody else knows that. A horse has to be claimed before a race, not after it."

"There's still that risk of losing him."

"But it's such a small one, Emmie. The advantages of him winning and going up in class outweigh it."

"You wouldn't enter your precious Boy Wonder in a claiming race, would you?"

"I don't have to. He's a stakes horse. Thunder doesn't meet the qualifications to enter the kind of races Boy runs. He's not in the same class yet, Emmie. Try to understand that."

She shook her head. "I don't want to risk losing him."

"Would you stop saying that!" Chad took a calming breath and continued. "Listen, honey. I know what I'm doing. All my other partners understand that and give me free rein to enter horses in any type of race I choose."

But Emily hoped she meant more to Chad than his other partners. She swallowed her pride. "Will you please withdraw Thunderbolt from this race for me, Chad? As a personal favor?"

His eyes blazed. His patience had come to an end. "Dammit, Emmie, that's not playing fair. I'm not going to scratch Thunder just because you think of him as a pet instead of an investment. Unless that horse can pay his way, he's useless to me."

"God, you're a hard man," Emily said.

"Only when it comes to business." He made a motion to touch her hair again.

She snapped back her head. "No, not only business. You wouldn't even talk to your poor father." She turned on her heel and went inside, slamming the screen door behind her.

"Don't waste your pity on King Barron," Chad shouted after her. "He's a hell of a lot tougher than I am."

She didn't respond, so he went inside to continue the discussion. He realized that she considered it over when he found her packing her bag in the bedroom.

"You're not leaving," he told her.

It was the wrong thing to say. "Just watch me."

He changed tactics. "Please stay."

"I need time to think this over by myself."

"I'll leave you alone. I'll go take a long walk."

"Off a short pier, I hope," she muttered.

That was a good sign, he thought. She was showing a little sense of humor about this. If he could get her into his arms he knew he could coax her into a more reasonable attitude. He moved toward her as slowly, as carefully as he would a skittish horse. "Emmie," he said in his deep soothing voice. "Come here, honey."

She fell to the floor and stuck her head under the bed.

Lord, she really was upset, Chad thought, not sure how to handle her now. But then he realized that she was just getting her cat, who took refuge under the bed anytime Chad came within ten feet of him.

"Sachet hates it here," Emily said, getting up again with the cat cradled in her arm.

"He'll get used to the smell of horses."

"Well, I don't think I can get used to the smell of a *rat*."

"I'm not even going to take offense at that, honey. We all tend to say things we don't mean when we're out of sorts."

Her golden eyes were like fireballs when she glared at him. "Don't you dare patronize me, Chad Barron. Either you promise to withdraw Thunderbolt from that race or I leave."

"Don't *you* dare give me ultimatums. I won't tolerate that from any woman."

Emily yanked her bag off the bed and walked out on him. He'd intended to tell her he didn't tolerate that from a man, either, but she hadn't given him the chance.

Chapter Twelve

Emily knew that she looked terrible after her sleepless night. What bothered her was that she *cared* how she looked. She cared because Chad would be seeing her. Contact with him was unavoidable if she wanted to visit Thunderbolt before his race. And she had to do that. It could be the last time she would have that right.

She was grateful that Flo had agreed to meet her at the track today. "How does this claiming business work exactly?" Emily asked her as they walked to the paddock area together.

"The claim has to be made fifteen minutes before post time, but it's secret," Flo replied. "So no one knows which horses are claimed prior to the race."

"What if the horse loses? Does it get claimed away?"

"Sure. Or if it wins. Or breaks down on the track. Just so long as the horse leaves the starting gate, the claimer has to take it for the established price, no matter what condition it ends up in."

"Then I hope Thunder refuses to leave the gate again."

"That's not the attitude to have, sweetie," Flo said, breathing a little hard with the effort of keeping up with Emily's long stride. "We want Thunder to win this race. A twenty-grand purse isn't exactly small potatoes, you know. Besides, the odds are against him being claimed."

"You sound like Chad," Emily said in an accusatory tone.

"I'll take that as a compliment," Flo replied. "Chad's a master at the claiming game. Nothing ventured, nothing gained—that's his motto."

"But he's gambling with a horse I care deeply about! I had hoped that would make a difference to him." Emily laughed bitterly. "That shows what a fool I am."

Flo looked at her closely. "You're in love with him, aren't you?"

"I thought I was." Emily shook her head. "I thought he felt the same about me. But now I'm not so sure."

"You'll feel much better after the race," Flo said. "My prediction is that everything will work out fine. Your problem is that you worry too much, sweetie."

No, Emily thought, her problem was that she had fallen in love with Chad Barron. All he cared about was winning, the personal losses be damned.

* * *

"He's looking good," Chad said to Moss, stepping back to admire Thunderbolt after saddling him.

"But you sure ain't," his foreman replied. "Rough night?"

Chad ignored his question. "I already discussed racing strategy with Budenberry. We're going to keep it simple, the way we do with Boy. Take the lead and keep it."

"Maybe all the special attention you've been giving him is gonna finally pay off," Moss said.

"That's what it's all about, Moss. The payoff."

Chad felt the hairs on his neck rise up and turned around. Emmie had arrived. She looked so pale, he thought. And so damn beautiful. He'd ached for her all last night.

"So you decided to come see the race," he said brusquely.

She didn't bother answering him. She addressed the horse instead. "How you doing, Thunder?" She went up to the colt and stroked his neck. "How's my darling?"

"Her darling," Chad muttered.

Meanwhile, Moss's craggy face had realigned to adjust into a smile. He directed it at Flo. "That's a mighty pretty hat you're wearing today, Purple Lady."

"Since when are you such a fashion expert?" she replied, but she looked pleased by his compliment. "Is Thunder going to win for us today?" she asked Chad.

"If he doesn't, I'll eat your hat."

Flo laughed. Moss laughed.

Emily didn't. "Good luck, Thunder," she said. She kissed his muzzle and stalked off.

Chad swore under his breath. "Moss, take over from here," he said in his next one, and went chasing after her.

He caught up with Emily just as she was leaving the private paddock area and disappearing into the milling crowd on the other side of the fence.

"Emmie, wait!" He grabbed her arm so that she wouldn't have any choice in the matter.

"Yes, what is it?" she asked coolly, looking down at his big hand gripping her upper arm.

"What's happened between us?" Chad asked her point blank.

"You tell me, Chad. I thought you cared about me."

"I do! I love you, dammit!" He was dimly aware of people turning to stare at them and lowered his voice. "What I feel for you has nothing to do with this race, Emmie."

"It has *everything* to do with it. Don't you understand? If I lose Thunderbolt today, I'll be losing the only connection I have with my father."

"Your father would have understood my position," Chad told her.

"That's right. He was a gambler like you! He didn't care about anything else."

"Emmie, don't confuse the issue. When I entered Thunderbolt in this race, I made a sound business decision. Once he proves himself, he can go up a notch in class and qualify for allowance races with bigger purses. If we gamble a little today, we can win a lot in the future."

"No more claiming races?"

"That's the goal."

How she wanted to believe him. To trust him. How she wanted to feel the security of his strong arms around her once again. Was that a weakness? Perhaps. But she was only human.

"Oh, Chad, I've been so miserable." She leaned against him and he enfolded her in his embrace. "The suspense is killing me," she muttered against the soft fabric of his shirt.

"You won't lose Thunderbolt, honey. It's going to be all right," Chad assured her, kissing the top of her head, stroking her back, soothing away her concerns.

But he couldn't quite soothe away *all* her concerns. As much as Emily wanted to believe that the outcome would be happy, the element of risk still disquieted her. She stiffened as the bell clanged and the horses broke from the gate. Chad released her and they both gripped the paddock fence as they watched the horses stream by in a roaring rush. Thunderbolt was leading the pack!

He ran his heart out from beginning to end, and Emily observed his magnificent performance in dazed awe. Only one horse challenged him at the last furlong, but Thunderbolt pushed past him and went on to finish first.

"I knew he could do it!" Chad yelled, showing uncharacteristic emotion.

He lifted Emily up by her waist and twirled her around. Her head spun. Her heart spiraled. Her body melted into his when he put her down again, but the moment she regained her balance she pulled back from him.

She pulled back so quickly that Chad had to shuffle his big, booted feet to regain his own balance. "What's wrong, Emmie. We *won!*"

"Are you forgetting?" she asked him, controlling the urge to grip him by his broad shoulders and shake him into remembering. Concern for Thunderbolt cried out like a lost child to her, yet all Chad seemed to care about was winning. "We have to find out if he was claimed or not!"

Chad shook his head and offered her an indulgent smile. "You're worrying for nothing, honey. No-body's gonna claim a maiden for that price. Come on. Let's go congratulate our horse and take him back to the barn. Then we'll have us a private celebration party. How does that sound?"

It sounded too good to be true, but Emily did her best to return his smile. Her uneasiness increased as they pushed through the crowd and went back inside the fenced-in paddock area.

She saw Thunderbolt at the opposite end of the paddock. He'd already been unsaddled and Moss had a hold of his reins. Moss was talking to another man. Emily recognized him as the trainer who had called Thunder a donkey.

"Wait here," Chad ordered her.

"Why?"

"Please, Emily. Let me go find out what's going on. I'll be right back."

Emily had no desire to follow him. She didn't want her worst fears confirmed. She watched from a dis-tance as Chad approached the other trainer. Their conversation was brief.

Chad turned and walked back to her and Emily had the sensation that he was walking toward her in slow motion, as if in a dream. A nightmare. She stayed frozen on the spot, ice running through her veins.

He didn't have to speak when he reached her. His eyes told her everything she didn't want to hear. But he said it anyway. "We lost him, Emmie. We lost Thunder."

"We?" she cried. "No, *you* did, Chad. Damn you, this is all your fault."

"I did what I had to do," he said calmly. "It was a justifiable risk."

"Was it worth it, Chad. Was winning worth losing everything?"

"We didn't lose everything, Emmie," he countered. "We won a sizable purse. And Thunder's claiming price was twenty-five thousand."

"You're right, Chad. You're always right. All you lost today was a horse." She took a deep ragged breath. "And me."

He shook his head. "I don't believe you. You still love me."

Emily couldn't deny it. "I'll get over it," she said instead. "I'll have to, now that I realize you don't love me enough."

"I've never loved a woman more," he told her.

"Then why didn't you withdraw Thunder from this race for me? I *pleaded* with you."

His face became rigid despite the emotion brimming in his eyes when he looked at her. "You can't ask me to prove my love by going against my principles, Emmie."

"I'll never ask anything of you again," she promised him in a sad, empty voice. "Goodbye, Chad."

Chad watched her cross the paddock, her head held high, her shoulders back. She maintained her dignity as she wrapped her arms around Thunderbolt's neck, pressed her cheek to his face, and then stepped aside so that his new owner could lead him away. She shook Moss's hand and left, too, going out the side gate without looking back.

Chad didn't follow her. He had made his position clear. She had rejected it. He felt awful about losing Thunderbolt, partly because the horse had potential but mostly because Emily had grown so attached to him. But you had to be tough in the racing business. Emily just wasn't tough enough. And that was too damn bad. He wasn't going to go down on his knees and beg her forgiveness for doing his job. No way. Chad was resolute in his belief that he had done the right thing. Now it was up to Emily to come around to his way of thinking.

And if she didn't? Chad took a deep breath. All he knew for sure was that he would not allow a woman to interfere with the way he ran his stable. He marched to it now. He tried to ignore the sudden emptiness in his heart by reminding himself how tough he was. But the emptiness almost overcame him completely and made him feel like nothing.

"I've never known you to be off your feed before, Chad," Moss commented as they sat in the track cafeteria a week later. "If you was a horse, I'd have Doc Revera check you out for colic."

Chad remained silent. He hadn't had much to say the past several days.

"Doc sure looks happy lately, doesn't he?" Bobby Lee commented, spiking one of Chad's french fries with his fork.

"Marriage to Jenny must agree with him," Moss said. "Mighty fine jockey, that Jenny. Females have a nice way with racehorses."

Bobby almost choked on the fry. "All you used to do is crab about her, Moss. Remember when she rode Thunderbolt and—" Bobby caught himself. "Sorry, Chad. Didn't mean to bring up a sore subject."

"What's so sore about it?" Chad growled. "We've lost horses in claimers before."

"Right," Bobby said agreeably but quickly changed the subject anyway. "Since when are you so gung ho on female jocks, Moss?"

"The Purple Lady's been sort of influencing my way of thinking concerning women," he admitted. "I'm mighty glad she still comes around the backstretch. I was worried she'd stop visiting after we lost Thun—" He also caught himself and shot a wary glance Chad's way.

Chad banged his big fist on the Formica table, spilling everybody's coffee. "Would you two stop tippy-toeing around the subject of Thunderbolt like balky ballerinas? I made the right decision when I entered him in that claimer. Considering Thunder's record, nobody in his right mind should have bought him off us for that ridiculous price."

"Unless he was a rival trainer with an ax to grind," Moss muttered.

"Yeah, Laker did it for spite," Bobby said. "To get back at Chad for snatching some winners off him in the past."

"That's the way the game's played, boys," Chad said wearily. He hadn't been sleeping very well lately.

"But we'll have the last laugh," Moss said. "I heard through the grapevine that ole Thunder acted up in his stall and injured his leg. Doc Revera advised Laker to keep him off the track for at least a month."

Chad narrowed his eyes. "That's nothing to laugh about, Moss."

"Thunder's injury ain't," Moss said quickly. "But the fact that Laker can't race him sure is." He made his barking sound.

"If that's the case, Laker's not following the vet's advice," Bobby said. "I heard that Thunder's running in another claimer today. Last minute entry."

"Why the hell didn't you tell me that?" Chad demanded.

The boy looked confused. "But I just did, Uncle Chad."

Chad attempted to look less fierce. "What race is Thunder entered in, Bobby?"

"The third, I think."

Chad checked his watch and immediately rose.

"Are you gonna do something foolish because of that curly-haired gal?" Moss asked him.

Chad left without replying. Moss slurped a last swallow of coffee, got up from the table and followed him out of the cafeteria.

They walked together to the paddock and observed Thunder from the sideline as he warmed up in the walking ring.

"His left front leg is the injured one," Chad told Moss. It took a sharp eye to notice that he was favoring it, however. Thunderbolt didn't seem to be in any pain.

"Must be shot full of bute," Moss said.

Chad nodded, his expression grim. Moss was referring to phenylbutazone, a drug used to alleviate soreness in horses. When a horse ran on bute, it moved freely because the equine anti-inflammatory alleviated the pain of the injury. Bute shut down the animal's warning system, however, and feeling no pain, the horse could injure itself further as it ran. Even though bute was legal, Chad believed it was responsible for the increase of breakdowns on the track, and he was dead set against using it on his own horses before a race. But Thunderbolt wasn't his anymore, and there was nothing he could do about the situation now.

The way Emily had looked the last time he'd seen her flashed in his mind once again. There had been such hurt and disappointment in her golden eyes, and he had been the cause of it. And for what good reason? To win, of course. Chad shook his head with regret. He had managed that just fine and lost Emmie in the bargain.

What would his father have done in his place, Chad wondered. And the thought suddenly dawned on him that it didn't matter what King Barron would have done, or what he would have thought of his only son's actions. It no longer mattered to Chad that his father had predicted his failure, and he no longer felt the great need to prove King wrong by surpassing his accomplishments. Those things no longer mattered because Emmie mattered so much. Chad realized with a clarity as sharp as the point of a knife that no success he could ever obtain would make him feel as complete and happy as Emmie could. And all the races he could win in the future—hell, even the Kentucky Derby—could never make up for losing her.

Moss nudged him with a sharp elbow. "Hey, you okay, Chad?"

"Let's just say I could use a good shot of bute myself to ease the pain."

"That don't sound good," his foreman said. He ruminated around a big wad of tobacco for a moment as he continued to observe Thunderbolt. "Runnin' on a weak leg like that could surely be a good horse's downfall," he finally proclaimed. "Anyone who claims Thunder today would be a damn fool."

Chad remained silent. Risking Emily's love had made him feel the biggest damn fool in existence.

Grateful that she didn't have any more appointments for the day, Emily opened her desk drawer and removed a transistor radio. She had gotten into the habit of listening to the afternoon broadcast from Pacific Downs Racetrack every afternoon for the past week. It was her only connection with Chad now.

She missed him terribly. Yet pride would not allow her to contact him. Chad had proven how little he valued her love when he'd lost what had been so precious to her. Or had she used Thunderbolt as an excuse to break with Chad because she feared he would eventually break with her? Emily found herself wondering about this more and more since they'd parted. Doubts about her own motivations made her uneasy. Perhaps she hadn't opened her heart to Chad as completely as she could have. Was comparing him with her father another form of self-protection? The more Emily thought about it, the more confused she became.

Her everyday existence seemed so tame and predictable compared to the backstretch life she had come to appreciate more and more. She turned on the radio, keeping the volume low as she worked on some tax guides for a client.

Only half-listening, Emily heard Thunderbolt named as an entrant in the third race. She turned up the volume, a rush of adrenalin making her heart beat faster.

"They're off!" the announcer called, and Emily leaped up from her chair. Pacing her office, she listened intently as the announcer described the race, but the only horses he mentioned were those in front. Thunder wasn't one of them. And then he cried out, *"A horse is down! Number six has collapsed. Thunderbolt."*

Blood rushed through Emily's ears, a deafening roar. When she could hear again the announcer was saying, in a restrained voice, that the jockey had walked off the course uninjured but the horse was being carted away in the animal ambulance.

Emily stared at the radio, horrified. She could hardly believe what she'd heard. When her assistant came into the office with a question, she frantically waved her away, afraid she would miss more information. After a few commercials, the announcer came back on the air and began discussing the upcoming race as if nothing had happened.

As if *nothing* had happened to her precious horse! Was Thunderbolt so badly injured that he would have to be— *No!* Emily slammed her mind shut to such a possibility. She would remain calm, drive to the track and find out what his injuries were. She would not allow herself to think the worst.

Chad found Emily slumped down in Thunderbolt's empty stall. His heart almost broke at the sight of her there, looking so miserable. He knelt beside her and held her limp hand. "So here you are, honey," he said softly. "Bobby told me you were somewhere in the barn."

"I've been waiting for you for over an hour, Chad." Her voice was barely audible.

"I'm sorry, Emmie. I was with Doc Revera."

"No one around here knows what Thunder's condition is."

"How did you hear about the accident?"

"On the radio."

"That must have been tough. But I'm thankful you didn't actually see it happen."

She gripped his hand. "Was it awful?"

"It's always awful when a horse breaks down on the track, Emmie. All that power and beauty falling into a crashing heap. You never get used to seeing it."

The color drained from Emily's lips and she squeezed his hand even tighter. "Tell me straight, Chad. Is Thunder dead? Did he have to be destroyed?"

"No! Poor Emmie, is that what you were thinking all this time?" He adjusted his position and cradled her against him.

"I tried not to but I couldn't help it." She pressed her head against Chad's solid chest and breathed him in. His scent was like life itself to her.

"Thank God no bones were fractured," he said. "He tore some tendons pretty bad, though." He sighed. "Real bad, I'm afraid. The smartest thing to do would be to retire him early. If not, he'll keep injuring that leg."

"Then I pray his new owner won't race him anymore."

"She won't. She's a real softy." Chad kissed the top of Emily's head. "Looks like you got Thunderbolt for a pet after all, Emmie."

"What?" She pulled away to look at him.

"I claimed him before the race, honey. For you. I went against all my natural horse sense and better judgment, and most likely I'm the laughing stock of Pacific Downs right now."

"You don't see me laughing, do you?" Emily began weeping instead.

"Hey, I did this to make you happy."

"I know," she sobbed. "Oh, Chad, I was wrong to expect you to prove your love by withdrawing Thunder from the race last week." She looked at him, her eyes glistening with tears. "I confused issues that should have been kept separate."

"And I didn't appreciate your feelings enough," Chad said. "I should have been more patient, more understanding. Instead, I went into my dictator act."

"But I was being just as dictatorial, darling. Thunderbolt came to represent too much to me. I kept forgetting I only owned twenty per cent of him."

"He's all yours now, Emmie. One hundred per cent. Maybe when you learn how to ride you can win some ribbons with him."

"Oh, Chad, I can't accept such an expensive gift from you." She wiped at her eyes, overcome by his generosity.

"Would you accept an engagement ring?" He laughed at her stunned silence. "I know you said we should take it one step at a time, Emmie. But I'm more a jumper myself."

"And *you* said you didn't have the time to make a commitment, Chad."

"I never did until you came into the picture, honey. I need you to give my life balance and meaning. I didn't realize that, until you walked out of it last week. I won some pretty major races during that time and the victories were like dust in my mouth. Want to know why?"

She touched his mouth with her fingertip, outlining its bold, sensual shape. "Tell me why, Chad."

"Because you weren't there to share them with me. Marry me, Emmie. Marry me soon."

Emily looked at him in the shadowy light of the stall. How perfect that he would propose to her here, she thought. "Yes, Chad, I'll marry you," she told him.

His dark eyes filled with joy. "Can we announce it at my father's birthday party?"

"Of course." She smiled her approval. "I'm glad you've decided to make up with him."

"Yep. It's time. That's another thing I realized when I feared I lost you, Emmie. It's time I forgot about my past differences with my old man and got on with my own life. Besides, you make me too happy to stay angry with anybody, honey. Even him."

"Your father really isn't so terrible, is he, Chad?"

"Well, my mother and my sisters all adore him and you probably will, too. He's got a mighty charming way with the ladies."

"Like father, like son," Emily murmured.

Chad didn't seem to mind the comparison. He stroked her face with lingering tenderness as he gazed into her eyes. "So when was it you decided you loved me, Emmie? I mean, when did you know for sure?"

"Oh, it was quite subtle," she replied. "I got struck by lightning one day."

Chad laughed. "We both got struck, didn't we? Pow! It ripped through the sky and tore through all our defenses."

"We didn't stand a chance," she agreed happily.

They kissed and heard the crack of lightning again, even though it was a perfectly clear, sunny day.

* * * * *

This April,
Silhouette *Special Edition* is pleased to present

ONCE IN A LIFETIME
by Ginna Gray

the long-awaited companion volume to her bestselling duo

Fools Rush In (#416)
Where Angels Fear (#468)

Ever since spitfire Erin Blaine and her angelic twin sister Elise stirred up double trouble and entangled their long-suffering brother David in some sticky hide-and-seek scenarios, readers clamored to hear more about dashing, debonair David himself.

Now that time has come, as straitlaced Abigail Stewart manages to invade the secrecy shrouding sardonic David Blaine's bachelor boat—and creates the kind of salty, saucy, swashbuckling romantic adventure that comes along only once in a lifetime!

**Even if you missed the earlier novels,
you won't want to miss**

ONCE IN A LIFETIME #661

Available this April, only in Silhouette *Special Edition*.   OL-1

IT'S A CELEBRATION OF MOTHERHOOD!

Following the success of BIRDS, BEES and BABIES, we are proud to announce our second collection of Mother's Day stories.

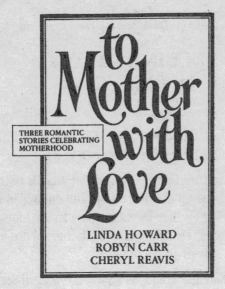

to

Mother

THREE ROMANTIC
STORIES CELEBRATING
MOTHERHOOD

with

Love

LINDA HOWARD
ROBYN CARR
CHERYL REAVIS

Three stories in one volume, all by award-winning authors—stories especially selected to reflect the love all families share.

Available in May, TO MOTHER WITH LOVE is a perfect gift for yourself or a loved one to celebrate the joy of motherhood.

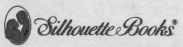 *Silhouette Books*®

ML-1

Silhouette Books®

SILHOUETTE BOOKS ARE NOW AVAILABLE IN STORES AT THESE CONVENIENT TIMES EACH MONTH

Silhouette Desire and Silhouette Romance

> May titles: April 10
> June titles: May 8
> July titles: June 5
> August titles: July 10

Silhouette Intimate Moments and Silhouette Special Edition

> May titles: April 24
> June titles: May 22
> July titles: June 19
> August titles: July 24

We hope this new schedule is convenient for you. With only two trips each month to your local bookseller, you will always be sure not to miss any of your favorite authors!

Happy reading!

*Please note: There may be slight variations in on-sale dates in your area due to differences in shipping and handling.